A CHINESE PERSPECTIVE

Brian Aldiss OBE was a fiction and science fiction writer, poet, playwright, critic, memoirist and artist. Born in Norfolk in 1925, after leaving the army Aldiss worked as a bookseller which provided the setting for his first book, *The Brightfount Diaries* (1955). His first published science fiction work, the story 'Criminal Record', appeared in *Science Fantasy* in 1954. Passing away in 2017, over the course of his life Aldiss wrote nearly 100 books and over 300 short stories – becoming one of the pre-eminent science fiction writers of the 20th and 21st centuries.

T0318043

BRIAN ALDISS

A CHINESE PERSPECTIVE

HARPER
Voyager

Harper*Voyager*
An imprint of HarperCollins*Publishers* Ltd
1 London Bridge Street
London SE1 9GF

www.harpercollins.co.uk

HarperCollins*Publishers*
1st Floor, Watermarque Building, Ringsend Road
Dublin 4, Ireland

First published in Great Britain in 1978 by Charles Scribner's Sons

This paperback edition published by HarperCollins*Publishers* 2021

A catalogue record for this book is available from the British Library

ISBN: 978-0-00-841259-3

This novel is entirely a work of fiction.
The names, characters and incidents portrayed in it are the work of the
author's imagination. Any resemblance to actual persons, living or dead,
events or localities is entirely coincidental.

Typeset in Sabon Lt Std by Palimpsest Book Production Ltd,
Falkirk, Stirlingshire

Note on the text

The text of this edition was generated by scanning earlier print copies of the story in its first edition. The text is a product of its period and presented here as it was in its first publication.

I

The tanks were of glass, a metre deep and almost as generous in their other dimensions. Each table contained eight tanks, and the laboratory contained ten tables. A constant temperature of 18.5 degrees Centigrade was maintained in every tank. And in every tank, oxygenators blew a chain of bubbles up their sides.

The water was of a different green in each of the tanks on a table, ranging from a pale stramineous yellow to a deep mid-viridian. The tanks were lit in such a way that watery reflections moved across the ceiling of the lab.

This perpetual underwater movement was lethargic. It lent the room a drowned and drowsy aspect in contrast with the dance taking place in all eighty tanks, where marine creatures of graded size underwent the capers of growth, performing such antics as their limited gene-patterns allowed.

Among this incarcerated activity went the Chinese girl who was known here as Felicity Amber Jones, neat in her orange lab coat, content because at present absorbed completely in her work.

The laboratory of which Felicity Amber Jones had charge was a part of the great institution of Fragrance Fish-Food Farms Amalgamated. The FFFFA, whose premises, buried deep into the plastic core of Fragrance II, produced one of the chief exports of the planetoid – a range of marine food-products famed all round the Zodiacal Planets. Those exports, packed in glass, plastic, or palloy, circulated in their various forms throughout the artificial worlds much as the free-swimming forms of oysters travelled through Felicity's ranged algae tanks on their way to maturity.

When it was time to go off duty, she registered the event on the computer-terminal in her office. Although she had plenty of other interests, Felicity always left this, her Main Job, with some regret. There was more peace here than at home in her cramped pile-apt. She switched off the overhead lights. The tanks, vats, and separators still glowed, spreading a languid jade reflection through the room.

At the changing-lockers, she removed her coat, standing naked for a moment before assuming a saffron overall, sokdals, and flesh mask. She called farewell to some passing colleagues as she made for the nearest exit.

Outside, someone had scrawled BANISH IMPERMAN-ENCE on the wall. Felicity made a moue at it and caught a petulent. In the moments of travel, she tried some astro-organic thought, but was too highly strung. It was almost time for her weekly assignation with Edward Maine, the great inventor.

II

In a homapt near the heart of Fragrance II, Fabrina Maine and her friend Anna Kavan stood before a small mock-fire. Its patterns cast themselves upon the legs of the two women in scarlet and gold, although they were over-shadowed by the gleaming wall-screen which Fabrina was now addressing.

Fabrina was a small plump lady whose wispy fair hair stood out unfashionably round her head; but she had a certain dignity. In an effort to improve that dignity, or otherwise express herself, she was currently studying Tease Structure, the psycho-dynamics of altered body-image. She adopted a vernal sacrifice position and said to the reporter on the screen, 'Yes, of course I can provide referents of my brother Edward's behavioural drives – none better than I – but that may not be convenient. First, you should introduce yourself. Which zeepee are you from?'

The reporter, looming easily on the screen and dwarfing the apartment she shared with her brother, said, 'My name's Sheikh Raschid el Gheleb, and I represent the *UAS Daily Modesty*. I've come up from Earth to investigate new techno-philosophical developments in the zeepees. So of course your brother ranks highly on the list of those people whom I hope to interview for my scatter.'

She frowned. Edward's increasing success brought increasing interruptions to their snugly predictable lives.

'Your Main Job?' she asked the reporter.

'On Earth, we don't have that same concept, although the World State Employment Council is studying its possibilities. I'm just the *Modesty*'s technophilosophical correspondent – though I do also lecture in Predestination at Cairo University. I hope you don't feel xenophobic about me just because I'm from Earth; we're very interested in the zeepees, you know.'

She sniffed. 'We manage very well without outside interference. Edward will be back later. Ring another time. You'd better speak to him direct. In any case, he has an Internal booked as soon as he gets home.'

She switched off and turned to Anna Kavan, leaning slightly towards the defile stance to show contrition. 'Perhaps I shouldn't have been sharp with him, but I'm uneasy about the thought of the World State meddling in our affairs, and so is Edward.'

'It's at least five years before the World State comes into being officially,' Anna said, extending her hands to the fake flames. 'Besides, the Chinese are very scrupulous.'

'Why should I care about the World State or the state of the world when I have my little lin with me?' Fabrina asked. She turned and petted the animated ornament by her side. 'Tell me something funny, Lin.'

'We are all radioactive particles in the mind of God,' said the lin. The women laughed.

'Now tell me a new story,' Fabrina said.

And the lin said, 'Here's one called "High Courts". There were high ideals in the courts upon the mountains. Photographers were scarce under the towering appletrees. No snails any longer laid their eggs among the eyes of the goats in the market. The Lady Cortara, that dinosaur of royal line, said, "Life is like death by drowning: it feels good when you cease to struggle." So worldly regiments failed to close the entanglement of minds.'

'You'll be able to afford a better model lin now, Fabrina,' Anna said. 'Edward will be rich from now on.'

'I happen to like mad old stories,' said Fabrina. 'And my little linikin's tales have the advantage of being original and sounding familiar.'

III

In the boardroom of Smics Callibrastics, high in the Fragrance II urbstak, they were celebrating Maine's achievement. Wine flowed, as well as the more customary aphrocoza, mitrovits, pam-and-lime, and other good things. The prototype of Maine's prediction machine stood at one end of the chamber; Edward Maine stood meekly by it, allowing the press to photograph him, and his colleagues to congratulate him.

'. . . and furthermore, I'd like to say, Edward, what a pleasure it has been to have you under our wing here at Smics for all these years,' Marvin Stein-Presteign told him. Stein-Presteign was Managing Director, and built for the job, with plenty of meat separating him from the rest of the world, topped by a florid enough countenance to remind that world that blood pressure and work pressure often run in alliance. 'Everyone enjoys working with you, Edward.'

'You're very kind, sir,' Maine said, smiling so energetically that his untidy fair hair, which stood out wispily all round his head, trembled in response. He was a small, plump man in his early thirties – clever but not very good at talking. Certainly not very good at talking to his meaty Managing Director.

Having shaken hands with Maine, Stein-Presteign moved away and said to Sheila Wu Tun, the Personnel Manager, 'There's no cynicism about Edward – he surely is a thoroughly admirable little man.'

'It's kind of funny the way everyone calls him Edward,' Sheila said. 'Never an Ed or a Ted or a Teddy . . . It's a factor of his rather remote personality, I suppose.'

'What's his private life like? Lives with his sister, doesn't he?'

'Yes. He's diffident with women, bless him. Although he has established a tentative relationship with a young woman who goes to his homapt once a week for an Internal.'

'Well, we have your little treat in store for him. Perhaps we can step up his fun-level there.'

'That's a thought – but Maine's entitled to be remote,'

Curmodgely from Statistics said. 'After all, the man is undeniably a genius.' He was rarely so bold with the Managing Director, but he disliked the patronizing way Stein-Presteign and Wu Tun spoke. He added with a note of apology, 'I mean, his damned machine *works*. The future is now foreseeable, more or less. It's going to change the history of mankind.'

Stein-Presteign said to Sheila, ignoring Curmodgely, 'I'll see Edward in my office tomorrow.' He moved on, leaving the lower echelons, who pressed admiringly if unavailingly round Sheila Wu Tun, to carry on the conversation.

Gryastairs of Kakobillis, who was heavy and eager, said, 'Luckily it was our organization which employed Maine and not the opposition. I suppose you all know that Gondwana of Turpitude have a patent on a destimeter which gives reliable predictions for up to thirty-six hours ahead?'

'It won't work as efficiently as our PM, Mr Gryastairs,' said a minor technician who had just joined the group. 'Our chance theories are much more sophisticated than theirs, for a start. The destimeter uses only superficial biochemical and physiological manifestations. There's no hormonal print-out. It was Maine's genius that he accepted right from the start that alpha-wave intensity is the key to reliable prediction, and for that you need constantly updated information-flow regarding hormonal activity and related data such as glucose-breakdown. The destimeter doesn't even take account of blood sugar levels, which to my way of thinking—'

'Quite so, quite so,' said Gryastairs heavily. 'Given the Chinese proof that Predestination can be the basis of an exact science, obviously you are going to get a number of approaches to the problem. Machines follow theory, as I always say. My point is simply that it was Smics Callibrastics who had the good sense to employ Edward Maine when everyone else regarded him as a crank. Now, we should have a marketable PM at least two years before the opposition. There's no ceiling to our potential selling platform.'

'I must talk to you about that,' said little Hayes of Marketing. 'It is going to be hellishly more difficult to promote and sell the product when the World State is established on Earth, and all their piddling new regulations and tariffs come into force—'

'Let's leave the World State out of the conversation just for tonight,' Curmodgely said.

While his confrères were talking shop, Edward Maine shook all the extended hands and smiled his simple smile. Occasionally he brushed his hair from his face, which was pink from several glasses of wine. With all the compliments ringing in his ears, he was very much the picture of a successful inventor; a slightly complacent smile hovered round his lips, while his manner was a little abstracted, as if even now he was elaborating his theory of non-randomness which lay behind the prototype PM.

The prototype resembled one of de Chirico's metaphysical figures mated with a small battery car. Maine was gazing not at it but at an immense painting which hung on the wall behind it.

The painting was the sole ornament on the walls of the Smics boardroom. It showed a strange feast taking place in the market square in a terrestrial country which might be Mexico or South America or Spain. A drunken peasant girl lay sprawled on a crude wooden table among the dishes; several men were feeling her while they ate and drank. Other people, men and women, stood round the table, laughing as they fed. Some of the men wore old raincoats. A skeleton was present, dressed as a monk.

Maine was interested in this central tableau. He also liked the way in which the picture was crowded with barrels and bright costumes and pots. The cobbles of the market square were vividly depicted. At the corners were further perspectives, a white-walled lane leading downhill, a cobbled stair leading up. The houses had tiles on their roofs. Maine supposed that such places must still exist on Earth, or else why paint them? Real things were amazing enough without inventing any more.

Out of habit, he began visualizing all the possible parameters of action implicit in the situation depicted on the canvas. The skeleton might signify that plague was about and that all present would soon die. Or further indignities might be heaped upon the drunken girl. Or the men might fight. Graphs of non-randomness flowed in his mind; where they intersected lay points of maximum possibility.

It would be wonderful to visit Earth again . . .

He felt the scale of the sundial under his wrist-skin. Seventeen-thirty. Soon time to get home for his Internal. Oh, that lovely girl! – If only he knew her externally! Well, at least there was that to look forward to.

Sighing, he turned and shook another extended hand.

IV

The last hand had come and gone. Maine caught the mainline home as usual, changing on to a graft and so to his own particular warren, deep among the braces of Fragrance. He hardly thought about the celebratory party which had been held in honour of his research team; his mind was on the pleasures to come.

'How did it go, Edward?' Fabrina asked. 'The party?'

'They were all very kind. It was a nice party. They are a pleasant firm to work with.'

'Mr Marvin Stein-Presteign?'

'Oh, yes, even Mr Marvin was there. He had quite a conversation, as the PM forecast.'

'Edward, did he – did he make you any kind of a *donation*?'

'Well, Fabrina, he made a speech. A eulogistic speech. Said that Western Civilization was not dead yet, and that we could still show China and the coming World State a thing or two . . .' He broke off, using his sister's visitor as an excuse to evade his sister's interrogation. 'Hello, Anna, how are you?'

'I'm just a radioactive particle in the mind of God,' Anna Kavan said, smiling, as she came forward and kissed Edward's cheek. 'At least, so your lin tells me. Why do you keep such an old-fashioned model, a man of your standing? You could afford some of the really intelligent ones, with up-to-date religious phobias and everything.'

'Like Fabrina, I enjoy our old lin. It's our pet. Anything too intelligent can't remain a pet. And the original idea of lins was to act as pet-substitutes, since live pets are not allowed in the zeepees.'

'You're both very eccentric,' Anna said. 'And I am going back to Earth very soon, where I shall purchase a Persian cat.'

'Some might think that was eccentric, Anna,' said Edward mildly.

Putting on her sentient extra face, she moved to the door. 'Edward, your innocence protects you from perceiving how eccentric I am. Stick to prediction and leave the squalor of human relationships to others.'

She blew them a kiss and left.

'What exactly did she imply?' Edward asked his sister.

'It's fashionable to talk in epigrams nowadays,' said Fabrina, who did not know either.

'Pretending she's about to go to Earth . . . People are always saying that, and they never go . . .'

Edward marched through into his own room, calling to the lin to follow him. The lin came in and stood itself against the wall until wanted, its plastic curlicues gleaming in the mock-firelight.

Among all the clutter of Edward Maine's hobby, which was also his Main Job, was his one extravagance. Most homapts, at least in the Superior group of zeepees, were equipped with funfaxes, for the reception of all media, including Internals. But Edward's was a two-way funfax. He could have his partner here with him.

Only in this vital respect had his shyness not entirely triumphed.

When the Intern-girl entered, shown in by Fabrina with proper courtesy and just a whiff of instinctive jealousy, she wore as usual a molycomp flesh mask, so that he had few visual clues to her real personality. She was dressed in a saffron tunic, with turn-up sokdals on her feet. There were white gloves on her hands. She bowed to him.

'You are well this week, Zenith?' he asked. Zenith was the code name they had agreed between them.

'Perfectly, thank you. As I hope you are.'

'Yes. And you still find happiness in your Main Job? With what is it connected?'

'My happiness is connected with artificial seas, thank you.'

Of course she assumed the Mandarin etiquette which was currently the rage on more progressive zeepees; so that she could only take her refusal to deliver a direct answer to a direct question – itself a breach of the Anonymous Internalizer contract – as far as a riddle. But the finesse she showed made him suspect that she was true Oriental.

As to her voice, it was low, but that meant nothing, for the molycomps often spread into pseudopods around the maxillae and sometimes down into the throat, altering the pitch of the voice in an attempt to baffle concealed voice-printers, just as her gloves baffled finger-printers.

'May I offer you an aphrohale before we go Internal?' he asked in a trembling voice. There she stood before him. He had but to reach out.

'It is better that we both defer to the terms of the contract binding us both, don't you think?'

'Of course, Zenith. As you wish. Apologies.'

Formal as a sarabande, they stepped one to one side of the funfax, one to the other. Edward pressed his face to the viewer, checking that the controls were set for his stipulated ride and the automap clued to the contracted region of her anatomy. He scarcely felt the hypodermic sting his ear lobe, or the hallucinogen course to the pleasure-centres of his hypothalamus. He had paid for a full twelve-week course with Zenith; this was week eleven; he was to venture into unknown, unvisited sectors of the girl he so terribly thought he loved only twice more.

V

Her thorax was a complex geography moving towards Edward through a syrup of ultraviolet. A great epidermal plain travelled beneath his view, its pitted inclines seemingly bereft of life, although the plain itself shuddered and vibrated like a wheat-field in storm. Gleaming, it rose to take in the universe; but the universe was illusion – at point of impact, the vertiginous plain melted and folded, revealing blue craters through which Edward's viewpoint – Edward himself – penetrated.

As he sank through her internscape, both magnification and rate of progress accelerated. The subcutaneous constellations of her sweat glands and adipose tissues fell upwards, entangled in pathways of vein and nerve fibre. Beyond them, barely glimpsed, were colossal geodesic structures which he recognized from previous journeys as an edifice of costal cartilege and rib – structural supports of the energy jungle he now invaded.

The wavelength was decreasing. As if the distant super-structure was a radio telescope trained on the violence of a far nebula, he was conscious of varying densities and materials working round him. Much of this material was as hostile to him as any pulsar emitting gamma rays. Immune, he sank further down into her unknown galaxies, at once penetrator and penetrated.

He passed unaware into the races of her thoracic aorta. There was no sensation of travelling down a tube, so congested was it, so packed with racing amorphous things – and every object packed with semi-autonomous intent. The intense ultra-violet magnification enabled him to see through the walls to vivid pulsations of energy beyond. They were at once like lightning and spaghetti. Everywhere, the disturbed and anonymous life of energy. He was merging with it. As the depth, the drug, took hold, he was no more than a rhythm in this tide of rhythmic impulses.

The predestined course wafted him timeless through galaxies of pancreas, duodenum, kidney, where renal syphonings regis-tered on his senses like ever-falling cascades of fire. From the boiling vat came a flood of grand spectral beings, lymphocytes and leucocytes, and the more meagre erythrocytes, pulsing yellow and mauve in colour, accompanying him down along the Amazon of the abdominal aorta and its deltaic offshoots.

Now the light was more subdued, the pace slower, the vanquishment of time and dimension more extensive. Now he was himself astro-organic – at once estranged from himself

12

and co-extensive with all being. Inarticulate outpourings of truth and life bathed him and radiated from him.

Beside him among the mute arterial ways was another resence: Hers, and yet something much more enduring than Her, a calm centre, which radiated back to him in dialogue the comforts he was involuntarily pouring out. It assured him of something for which his ordinary state of being had no vocabulary – something to the effect that this microcosm of body had no more to do with the whole human being than had the macrocosm of the starry universe, yet that both microcosm and macrocosm were intimately, intricately, non-randomly, related to the human . . . and there was a word there like psyche or soul . . . a non-existent word which possibly implied 'conundrum'.

And the Anima which teased him in a way that seemed lucid at the time – that Anima was as much of him as of her, a common spirit which perhaps, in similar circumstances, he might equally well have found in a leopard or a reindeer, a spirit born of all the mindless energy, yet itself calm, mindful.

It led him to one of the cable-like branches of the nervous system, where obscure messages rattled past him like lighted express-trains at night, carrying news of who-knows-what to who-knows-where. In the hypogastric system, lights were as jarring as sound, until he slipped away into a less frenetic area, resting in a rococo region of ligament and ramus patterned like a feather. The impetus of his voyage was dying. He floated there in stasis, knowing that soon tides over which he had no control would bear him back again to whatever condition he had relinquished.

At that, a sense of desolation seized him, but he threw it off in wonder at the splendid pelvic landscape surrounding him. The solemn structures among which he moved, bathed in low X-ray, had no macrocosmic equivalent, being at once gaseous formations, jungle growths, architecture. He became enclosed in a cathedral-like galactic lagoon, where nerve fibres stood out to meet him like roots of mangroves, welcoming him to the infinite confines of her vesico-uterine fold. There he stayed while a state much brighter than darkness fell, brooding like God over the measureless waters.

VI

When Edward found himself back to ordinary consciousness again, he was touched with disappointment. It was under the cloak of such characteristic melancholy that the girls who hired themselves out for Internals generally managed to vanish away, avoiding meeting their clients face to face.

As he sank into a chair, soaked and exhausted, Edward saw that his hired Zenith was going.

'One week more,' he said. He held his face with trembling hands.

'I will return next week.'

'Zenith – whatever your name is – stay a moment until I recover. Touch me!'

'You know the Contract.'

He looked at her desperately, and his gaze lit on the lin, standing silent against the wall.

'For courtesy's sake – for kindness – let my lin amuse you with a short tale! Lin, tell Zenith one of your stories.'

Before Zenith could say anything, the lin spoke.

'This story is called "Pacific Squalor". New taxation caused squalor in a Pacific town. "Weaving mills require a pretty sponsor," cried the citizens atrabiliously. But an airport was built and a sparkling bucolic comedy performed. All denied attempting to pervert justice. "Let fate no longer lead to loneliness," whispered the oldest lady. So patterned windows were built.'

'You have an old-fashioned lin,' said Zenith.

Edward wiped the damp hair from his forehead. 'You must know more about me than I about you. I am not rich.'

'I apologize for implied criticism. The story your lin has told pleases me.'

Every time, he had coaxed a little conversation from her. In pleasure now, he said eagerly, 'It really amused you?'

She stood before him, the molycomp mask smiling but expressionless.

'Didn't Anton Chekhov say that stories should not be about life as it is or as it ought to be but as it appears in dreams? Your lin's story is of that kind.'

'You know Chekhov's writings?'

'I make a close and interested study of European writing . . . I mean, that is one of my Side Jobs . . . Now please excuse me – I have over-stayed my time.'

In her tunic, her robe, her gloves, her mask, she went. Edward sat on his chair.

'Would you like a story or a joke?' asked the lin.

'No.'

She had made a slip there, definitely a slip. 'European writing' . . . that was not a phrase anyone of American or European stock would use about a Russian writer. Despite his French influences, Chekhov would be regarded as a European writer only by someone completely outside the European community. An Asiatic, for instance. He was more certain than ever that Zenith was Chinese. And after next week, he would never see her again. Contracts were non-renewable. The damage that Internals did to anyone submitting to them – damage that could ultimately result in death – shrouded the transactions in mystery and restriction. The Japanese, Edward recalled, had invented this ritual, investing it with all the formality of a tea-drinking ceremony.

Much as he might dislike that formality, he saw its point. The intimacy of a person-to-person Internal was such that it had to be guarded by formula. Otherwise he, at least, would have been too shy to face the confrontation.

'The Contract!' he said aloud. Always, he was bound by contracts, written or unwritten, whether to his firm or his sister, his landlord or his Internal-girl. With a flash of insight, Edward perceived that all men were similarly bound, whether they recogized it or not. Otherwise, his predestination machine would have no hope of working. The illusion of free will was simply a lubricant to keep the machine working smoothly.

He couldn't face it. Getting up, he staggered over to the aphrocoza bottle.

VII

The computer controlling the gyroscopes at the heart of Fragrance II kept the planetoid riding precisely in its orbit. That orbit was elliptical, with the planet Earth at one of its nodes, set at an angle of 83.45 degrees to the plane of the ecliptic, so that the sun's energy washed ceaselessly like an ocean about the speeding body.

In its eternal morning, Edward Maine woke to another manmade morning, accepted coffee from Fabrina (who offered it in the classical auspices stance), and staggered over to do his daily horoscope seated at the PM.

The analytics went into action, reading his basic physiological functions, such as pulse rate, hormone level, encephalic activity, tension index, and so on, and immediately the transmitter began a print-out.

The very first symbol on the paper caught Edward's attention. It showed that this was to be a day of prime magnitude. He had never received that signal before, except once – on the day they had been expecting it at Callibrastics, when the breakthrough came with the application of chance laws to personal data banks.

For a second time the analytics went into action, feeding Edward's response level into the computer, where it would be matched against all the background data plus the new data on all local events arriving during the artificial night of Fragrance. This double-check on response levels ensured that, by gauging Edward's current reaction to challenge, the day's reading of event-flow would be as accurate as possible.

The event-flow began to appear. The further ahead in the day, the less reliable the prediction. Possibility percentages were attached to each nodal event. All items were listed in likeliest chronological order, related in the PM's usual cryptic style.

```
**Key day. Surprise gift from corp mixed
     with contempt                              95
  View provides revelation on which future hinges 89
  Do not attach too much importance to self
  HL (Hormone Level) indicates sudden
     mind-change                                91
  Unsettling news. Fogginess. Presumption leads
     to quarrel with sister                     85.5
  Concealed beauty leads to religious argument  78
  Lack of lobster recognition interests         77
  Make simpler daily the beating of man's heart
  Priestly contact aids welfare approach        69
  Search yields nil result                      79
```

Summary: day of interest, many new possibilities

17

Edward sat looking at the print-out for a long while. Every line seemed to pose a fresh mystery, although that was the way with the PM prototype, even on a quiet day. The problem was often a simple semantic one: that to predict an event accurately, the terms had to be imprecise; conversely, when the terms were precise, the accuracy quota was forced down. Heisenberg's uncertainty principle ruled.

All the same, some of the factors were mildly staggering. 'Quarrel with sister'. Precise enough, but he never quarrelled with Fabrina. Then, 'Do not attach too much importance to self'. This contrasted with the machine's favourite homily, which was that Edward should attach more importance to himself. Advice instead of straight prediction generally indicated fuzzy set thinking, where the computer was unable to make any either-or evaluation, or else concealed a surprise factor determined by event-currents (in the jargon of Callibrastics) on which the computer had insufficient data. The final line sounded horribly downbeat, whereas the summary held ambiguous promise.

One thing at least was clear. He had a challenging day ahead. He took a timid shot of aphrocoza before heading for the elevator.

VIII

Edward spent the first hour of the morning with a calculator, trying to work out applicable Laplace formulations for human action. Once they developed a suitable tool for handling the equilibrium and motion of human life-flow, they would have a convenient way of making the PM smaller and more marketable. Edward believed that in a non-intermeshing event world, perturbations of behaviour would be periodic rather than cumulative; if Callibrastics could achieve a field-equation to cover this reaction, an all-applicable calculus of chance would do away with most of the tedious process of physiological function-reading which at present inaugurated every day's prediction.

Edward was deep in the work, and enjoying it, when Sheila Wu Tun poked her elegant face up on his screen and said, 'Edward, dear, would you mind going to see Mr Marvin Stein-Presteign, please?'

'Of course, Sheila.' He jumped up. Making sure that none of his assistants had their eye on him, he licked his hands and tried to straighten out his untidy hair. He adjusted his collar as he made his way to managerial level.

Surprise gift from company. Surely that could only be good.

Stein-Presteign was all smiles. He was a genial green colour. His office, as befitted the Managing Director of Smics Callibrastics, was set on the outside of the Fragrance Light Industrial pyramid. His window looked out over the edge of Fragrance before it fell away in sheer cliff, and the sun, blazing through the planetoid's dome, was toned down by chlorophylter shutters, whose output went to feed the riotous blooms of Stein-Presteign's indoor garden.

For a world that practised the formalities, Stein-Presteign was remarkably informal. He bowed as deeply as his solid bulk would allow and motioned his visitor to a chair.

Awed as ever in the presence of his boss, Edward sat meekly down to listen to a general preamble.

'The scatters are always telling us that we are through creatively,' Stein-Presteign said. 'The argument goes that the Renaissance was the period when Western man set his targets towards the next few hundred years. In Italy in the fifteenth century, rich middle-class families in Milan, Venice and Florence and such cities suddenly came out with dynamic ideas of humanism, individualism, and speculation about the material world. You could say that the Borgias and the rest of them were the early founders of those goals that led us to space travel.

'Then the movement spread outwards through Europe and so, eventually, to the Americas. Particularly to North America, although Brazil is now having her turn. But the general impression seems to have gotten around that, with the rise of China to world dominance and the dwindling of mineral and fossil oil deposits, the spirit of the Renaissance is dead.'

He put his fist down heavily on the desk, leaning forward and looking hard at Edward. 'I do not believe that the Renaissance is dead, Edward. I have never believed it. We have in you and your team here in Callibrastics proof positive that the old inventive enquiring spirit of Leonardo and the other guys lives on. The scatter-pundits fail to see that the general retreat of the brains of much of the Western world to the zeepees in search of free energy has caused a revolutionary regrouping. My firm belief is – I have stated this before and shall state it again, in defiance of defeatist thinking – that the zeepees duplicate in many essential ways the conditions of the Italian Renaissance cities. My belief is that Fragrance and the Ingratitudes – even Turpitude, for God's sake – are so many little Florences and Milans . . . Of course, the Italians didn't have the goddamned Chinese to deal with . . .'

The Managing Director followed up this last remark with a moody silence. Feeling something was required of him, Edward said, 'Of course, an argument by analogy—' but Stein-Presteign swept the puny sentence away with a new flood of talk.

'Well, I've been reviewing things in that light since I returned home from the party last night. Among the matters I reviewed was your pay structure, Edward, and it did occur to me that for a man as distinguished in his way as Leonardo da Vinci, you have not been treated entirely with the generosity for which Smics Callibrastics is rightly renowned, right? That is to say, not on a scale commensurate with the generosity of the merchant princes towards the painters, architects, and scientists they patronized. So I determined to make a gesture – a grand gesture that will perhaps fire you to greater things.'

'Really, sir, you're very kind, but—'

'Edward, the company is going to send you on vacation to Earth for a whole month. You need a vacation, and travel will broaden the mind. You have no damned personal life here worth speaking of. Well, we're going to send you down there—' he gestured eloquently towards the window '—to relax and refresh the springs of your mind, work up some more psychic energy. We pick up all the tabs, O.K.?'

Edward hesitated, and Stein-Presteign added, 'What's more, the vacation, including the space travel involved, is for two. So you can take that sister of yours along for company.'

Confused though he was, Edward registered the note of contempt in the director's voice. Unable to sit still, he got up and went to the window to hide the workings of his face. Taken at face value, the offer was terribly generous; but could he take it at face value? Stein-Presteign despised him. Were they trying to sack him?

Between elation and dismay, he stared out at the panorama of urbstaks marching towards the edge of Fragrance's disc. Maybe the planetoid was too small for him, although that was also one of its attractions; yet how wonderful to see the oceans again, as he had when a boy.

From where he stood he could see the far-ranging boxes of the administration of FFFFA, whose industrial levels went down into the core of Fragrance. Most of the planetoid's food was produced there – whereas on Earth he would be able to eat natural food again. A phrase floated to his mind: 'My happiness lies in artificial oceans . . .'

He turned about.

'I accept your kind offer. I'd love to be Earthside and stand on a shoreline watching the ocean again. I'll go.'

Pulling a solemn face, Stein-Presteign came round the desk and shook Edward's hand without speaking, looming over him as he did so. He laid a hand on his employee's shoulder and said, 'There's one point to take into consideration, Edward. We – you, I, Callibrastics, the whole of Fragrance – stand to get very rich from our PMs. We can sell 'em by the thousand among the zeepees and break even very comfortably, as I suppose you realize.

'But our real target must be Earth. We must be able to sell PMs on Earth. That's where the real market lies.'

'That shouldn't be hard,' Edward said. 'The Chinese have long believed in predestination—'

'You're being politically naïve, Edward.' He took a step forward, almost as if determined to crush Edward under his great prow. 'What the Chinese believe on that score is neither here nor there. What they do believe in is selling their own wares – just as we do, come to that. They're getting this World State into constitutional order, and there's no doubt they can set up destructive tariffs against us out here. Many of my friends believe that is one of the chief objects of World State. I don't myself. My belief is – I have stated this before and shall state it again – that the Chinese are good horse-traders. And that's where you come in.'

'I hardly know what a horse looks like,' said Edward, aghast.

'Holy gravities!' Stein-Presteign exclaimed, clutching his

forehead. 'I'm speaking metaphorically, son, metaphorically! Does the name Li Kwang See mean anything to you?'

'Apart from the fact that it's a Chinese name, no.'

'Li Kwang See is a very distinguished bureaucrat. He's served his time in the Peking government and now he's just been appointed Minister for External Trade, a post he takes up when the World State becomes reality. He has the usual prejudice of his kind against Western science. When you're on holiday, Edward, the company wants you to go round and call on Mr Li Kwang, and persuade him to like our PM.'

'You want me to—?' He was overcome by excitement.

'Callibrastics *trusts* you, Eddy.' Again the hand on the shoulder. '*I* couldn't be trusted to chat up Li Kwang. I'd be too heavy-handed. But your nice quiet little way of going about things . . .'

'All right. Of course I'll go and see him,' Edward said, breaking free of what threatened to be an embrace. 'I believe in the virtues of the PM probably even more than you do, sir. I certainly know more about its working. Some of these Chinese statesmen are very civilized men. If I can't sell it, nobody can, sister or no sister.'

He blushed, seeing himself in the diplomatic role. 'People were good enough to say last night what a pleasure it was to work with me – well, I will impress Mr Li Kwang favourably. We can get in before Gondwana and our other rivals. I can get him to order some machines. He'll know someone in the Internal Trade department – I'll come back with a big order, rely on me.'

'Of course, I have always admired your enthusiasm, Edward.' Stein-Presteign retired round the desk and gestured curtly to Edward's chair. 'It is best that we all know our capabilities and limitations. Frankly, you alarm me. You must understand that all we want you to do is to establish a friendly contact with Li Kwang, nothing more. When the time comes to sell, believe me, Edward, Callibrastics will send out its prime sales force on the job. Professionals, not amateurs. We certainly shall not rely on anyone in Research for such a delicate task . . .'

Seeing that he had been too crushing, he added, 'But yours will be the perfect touch to convince the Minister that our slice of Western science is fully in accord with Chinese principles, non-exploitive, non-imperialist, and so on. You're so obviously a non-imperialist character that you are our first choice for such a mission, right? O.K., get Sheila Wu Tun to assist you with any little problems. She has been briefed.'

Edward rose. 'You're extremely – I'm extremely—' He held out his hand, then he scratched his head with it. Then he left.

IX

He went back and stared at the flowers growing under the falsie in his office so much less prolifically than the flowers below the Managing Director's real window. He decided that he was trembling too much to do any creative work and might as well go home for the day.

Pleasant odours wafted through the carriage on the way home – someone had slipped their card in the Perfume slot – but he was restless and curiously upset. On the one hand, the corporation had been generous; on the other hand, they had tied a condition to the vacation and had been insulting. Of course, he deserved all he got, both the good and the bad. *You're too damned self-effacing for your own good*, he told himself. *And at the same time you think too much about yourself.*

He attached too much importance to self – at a time when

24

predestination brought the whole nature of self into question. That was something they'd never had to bother about in ancient Venice or wherever it was.

To his relief, the homapt was empty when he returned. At this time, Fabrina was at her job at the Fire Department. The lin was activated by his presence; it unplugged itself from its charge socket and came to him. Its simulated wrought-iron framework gleamed. It had dusted itself this morning.

'Your pleasure levels are low, Edward. Would you care for a story?'

'No.'

He tramped past it into his room and poured himself a large aphrocoza. The mixture of liquid and heavy gas rolled into his beaker like a slow wave. He poured it into mouth and nostrils, quaffing it back till all was gone. Then he felt slightly better.

The lin was standing meekly beside him.

'All right, all right!' Edward said. 'For g's sake, do your thing!'

'Here's a story called "Volcano Obliteration". Lorna put her hands conversationally round an old grey falcon,' the lin said. 'In the town, a silver band played, but she had heard too many promises. She cried, "I must return with honour to my father." But a volcano obliterated the valley. Now she lives with incredible leopards while a harlot plays "Flower Patterns" in her head. She attempts to mind the animals courteously.'

'Good, now go and plug yourself in again.'

'You have tired of my stories.'

'Emotional blackmail is something you weren't programmed for.'

Edward sat silent and glum, pouring more aphrocoza into himself and finally falling asleep in his chair, to undergo curious waking dreams which were dispelled when Fabrina entered the homapt.

He went through and said to her, 'I've just dreamed up the final proof of why God can't exist. Everything is predetermined; our more fortunate ancestors were able to believe in free will only because they did not understand that random factors are themselves governed by immutable laws.'

'You're home early, Edward. I've bought us a halibut steak for supper.'

'Everything was always predetermined. How could anyone big-minded enough to be God enjoy sitting back for countless aeons of years and watching what was to him a foregone-conclusion working itself out? . . . Of course, I suppose what seems such an incredibly long time to us may be just a flash to him. Maybe he has a lot of pin-ball machine universes like ours all spinning at once.'

'You've been at the aphrocoza, Edward. It always gets you on to ontology.'

'Maybe we could develop a computer which would prove conclusively whether or not God exists. No, that would hardly be possible – just as Karl Popper proved that no computer can predict the future that includes itself, although it can predict personal futures. Perhaps there are personal gods. Or maybe fully developed PMs will turn into personal gods . . .'

'Father used to say that God was much more dirty-minded than was generally allowed for.'

'There are limits to the possible. There must be a formula for those limits. It might be possible to compute those limits. But then, again, if we knew what the limits were, and how near we were to them, that would make the universe even more boring than it is now. Think how tired I am of my *own* limitations. I'm just a souped-up version of lin.'

26

She settled into a bending reed position and said dismissively, 'You know you like Lin's stories when you're sober.'

'Ah, ah, ha—' He waved a finger at her. 'But why do I like them? I enjoy their limitations. I enjoy the sense of being able to determine the limits of Lin's brain, of being able to encompass easily the farthest distance its story-patterns can reach. You don't mean to tell me God is as petty-minded as to enjoy our little patterns of circumstance in a similar way?'

'Has something happened to upset you?'

'There are those who might say that "orbitally-perturbed" was a better phrase than "upset", my dear, but – in a word, yes. I was up before Wine Stain this morning, and he has given me a month's vacation on Earth, to go wherever fancy takes me, to wander in the Rockies, to march to the sea . . . Thalassa! Thalassa!' There it was out!

Fabrina's pose collapsed. 'You shouldn't say such things, whether you're high or not. I try never to think or speak about Earth . . .'

He was startled at this. 'You don't hate Earth? Just because we hear how much it's changing!'

She looked up at him and then covered her eyes. 'Hate? I never said anything about hate. It's just that we've been on Fragrance for so long that I've ceased . . . I've ceased to believe anywhere else really exists. Fields, ordinary skies, irregular ground, wide horizons, trees – I can't imagine them any more. There's just these walls and the fake view out of the falsies, and the caverns and trafficways. Anything else is like – a Greek myth, I guess. I can't even believe in Death any more, Edward, you know that? I think we're doomed to go on here forever, unchanging.'

Edward went rigid, defending himself against what she was saying. 'Time goes too fast . . .'

'You only add to the imprisonment, Edward. Father always

said you lacked humanity . . . You spend your life trying to drag in the future to be more like the past, to make everything all the damned same . . .'

He moved over to her, leant over her, only to find himself unable to touch her, to do more than stare at her carefully turned shoulder.

'Fabrina, why are you talking this nonsense? What's the matter with you? Things are changing all the time! Are you really afraid of change? Didn't you hear what I just said? – Callibrastics has given me a vacation for two on Earth. That's good! You act like it was something awful.'

She looked up at him. He took a step back.

'You're not just fogged with aphrocoza? It's true? Oh, Edward, a whole month on Earth for the two of us!' She jumped up and threw her arms round him. 'I just thought you were lying, and I couldn't bear it. It reminded me how I hate this place. When do we go?'

'You don't hate this place. You have your friends here, every comfort.'

She laughed bitterly. 'O.K., you like it so much, you stay and I'll go. I'll take Anna – she's dying to get back!'

'Listen, Fabrina, you aren't invited yet.'

'I'm coming with you – you said so.'

Suddenly he was furious. His hair came quivering down about his eyes; he dashed it away. 'All I said was it was a vacation for two. I didn't say who I was taking with me. Why should it be you? Why do I have to have you round my neck all the time? If I want a holiday, then I'll take someone else. You're only my damned sister, not my wife, you know!'

They stood facing each other, slightly crouched, their hands rigid and not quite clenched, as if they were about to attack each other.

'I know I'm not your wife. I'm more like your servant. All these years I've looked after you! If you're going to Earth then you'll take me and nobody else.'

'I'll take whom I please.' But he weakened, recalling Stein-Presteign's contemptuous assumption that he would go with his sister because he had nobody else. Assumptions such as Stein-Presteign's and his sister's carried terrible power.

'You'll have to take me, Edward. What would people think if you didn't?'

This unexpected feebleness on her part strengthened him. 'I don't care what people think – this is something I've earned and I'm going to enjoy it. I'm going to take a woman with me, I'm going to enjoy myself. Just for once, I'm going to live. That's something you've never thought of.'

'What woman would have you? They'd laugh!'

'Little you know about women! Father always said you should have been a boy.'

'Don't bring that up! Let's not go into the past. The things our parents did to us are all over and done with. Father *wanted* me to be a boy, didn't he, because you were so flaming inadequate in the role, but that's not my fault. You were always his little pet, weren't you, and what went on between the pair of you was none of my business.'

'You tried to make it your business, just as you still try to interfere in all my relationships now. Besides, who was mother's little pet, eh?'

'Well, come on then, give – who was mother's little pet? It wasn't me, that's for sure. It was Alice, wasn't it, your favourite sister!'

'Leave Alice out of this, you bitch. She's dead too, and we both know what killed her.'

She hit him across the face.

He stepped back, raising his hand to his cheek, resting his knuckle on his lip and glaring at her across the edge of his palm.

'You're still lousy with guilt,' he said. 'It shows in everything you do. It settles like a blight on everything you touch.'

'If you're trying to blame your blighted life on me, think again. You may recall that it was you who persuaded me to come and live up on this miserable pseudoplanet.'

'More fool me!'

'Right, more fool you! You always were a fool.'

'I'm going out,' he said. 'I can't take any more of you!'

'And you're a coward, too!'

'Relax, I know you'd love to have me strike you and pummel you into a pulp. That's really what you want, isn't it? Not just from me, from any man!'

'You talk so big to me. You creep to all the real men in your precious Callibrastics, don't you?'

He went through into his room and sat on a chair to pull his sokdals on. As he came back through the main room to reach the outer door, she said, 'Don't forget Anna will be here at five.'

He left without answering. Unfortunately it was impossible to slam their airtight door.

X

Fragrance Fish-Food Farms Amalgamated presented a clear profile only when their administrative levels rose above mean city-level. Below that, successive storeys down mingled with the surrounding establishments and were interpenetrated by the mainlines and tunnels of the public transport system, so that they merged into the complex web of the city capsule. Most storeys nevertheless had a formal entrance as well as many functional ones, perhaps as a fossil of ancient two-dimensional approaches to urban planning, and it was at one of these formal entrances that Edward Maine presented himself.

Edward had a Brazilian friend in FFFFA called José Manuela do Ferraro, who worked in the Genetic Research department of the giant corporation. A neat little Japanese assistant came to meet Edward and escorted him to José's floor. She led among huge vats milling with young prawns and deposited him at the door of José's office.

The Brazilian was a big man, who jumped up and shook Edward's hand, clapping him on the back and smiling broadly.

'You're very successful nowadays, Edward – I saw a report of your celebratory party on the scatter. It makes you too busy to attend Tui-either-nor meetings, I guess?'

'Afraid so. Are you still a priest in your Side Job?'

'Can't afford to give up Main Job – besides, it fascinates me so. Come and see what we are doing in the Homarus division.'

'That's very kind, José, but—'

'Come on, we can talk as we go. I miss our arguments at Tui meetings, Edward. You were so good – you sharpened my wits. Now I suppose you work too much with computers to have any religious feelings.'

Edward had other matters than religion on his mind, so all he said, reluctantly, was, 'We need computers.'

'Agreed, we need computers at this stage of man's progress,' José said, opening a swing door for his friend. 'But progress should be towards the sciences of self-knowledge not towards technology-slanted sciences. That's a deadend. Even I have to work with computers in Main Job, while denouncing them in Side Job. We must think in fuzzy sets, not the old either-or pattern so basic to Western ideology.'

'I know, I know,' Edward muttered. 'But either-orness has brought us a long way.'

'Now we are being defeated by alien Chinese ways of thought. You must believe in my sub-thought. Sub-thought exists and is measurable – we are getting proof. Sub-t is much more random and instinctive than ordinary logical thought; it must not be structured like thought. Sub-t is related to will, and will, as we know, can modify neural patterns in the brain. If we believe in Freud, then we have Freudian dreams, and so on. If we believe in computer-human analogies, then we will come to think and sub-t like our machines. So we will be totally dominated by either-orness. Then all creativity will be lost.'

'Creativity always breaks out anew, every generation.'

'Yes, but unpredictably – even in your worlds of predestination, old friend! With Tui-either-nor, we can nourish it, make barren logic subject to creativity, rather than the other way round as at present.'

'That's putting it too strongly,' Edward said, with a feeble smile.

'No, it's not, not while the Western world is in recession generally. Tui is the old Mandarin symbol for water – a lake, for instance, signifying pleasure and fluidity. That's what we need, fluidity. Among all the religions of the zeepees, Tui is the only fructifying one, the only one that genuinely offers redemption – the redemption not just of one's self but of others!'

'I must try and get round to meetings again,' Edward said. 'Do you still make those ringing priestly addresses to God about Tui?'

'Of course.'

'And does God answer?'

José laughed good-naturedly. 'When you speak to God,

that's just prayer. When he starts speaking to you – that's just schizophrenia.'

They were walking among gigantic three-layered tanks in which large lobsters sprawled. The tanks were dimly lit, while the laboratory itself remained unlit. Yet it looked as if many of the lobsters could see the men, so quickly did they turn to the glass walls of their prisons and signal with antennae and claws, as if asking to be released.

'We are just beginning to realize how many kinds of thinking there are,' José said. 'Predestination works only for those who believe in it . . .'

'I feel bound to challenge that statement!' Edward exclaimed. 'After all—'

'Don't challenge it, remember it. Feel it fertilize you. I will show you how a little Tui thinking worked for us here.' They had come to a fresh series of tanks in which more lobsters sat. José changed the subject as smoothly as if he imagined he was still talking about the same thing. 'These lobsters that you see here are not much different from the ancestral lobster, *homarus vulgaris*. You can see they're a sort of dull reddy-yellow, spotted with little bluish-black patches. The only difference is that these chaps are bigger; they weigh up to six kilos. We have to breed 'em big, which we do in the traditional way of mixing inbred lines with crossbreeds for hybrid vigour. By using ideal temperatures, we can persuade them to grow to mature market size in two years rather than three.'

'Do you import sea water from Earth?' Edward asked.

'Genes, no – far too expensive, *and* sea water is not pure enough for our purposes. This is all artificial sea water – in fact, synthetic water in the first place, hydrolized out of hydrocarbons and oxides floating in space.'

He rapped against the glass. 'But you see the trouble with

ordinary lobsters. They're nasty pugnacious creatures, so aggressive that they have to live in solitary confinement throughout life, or they'd eat each other. Which puts up *per capita* costs greatly, when you consider that on Fragrance alone some twenty-three million kilos of lobster meat are consumed per annum – which means a lot of lobsters, and a lot of tanks.'

'I mustn't take up any more of your time,' Edward commented.

José took his elbow and led him back along the way they had come, where the rows of tanks were more brightly lit. Here, lobsters jostled together in apparent *bonhomie*, armour notwithstanding.

'These certainly are highly-coloured,' Edward said. 'I didn't recognize them as lobsters at first.'

'They don't recognize *each other* as lobsters,' José said. He beamed, and made embracing gestures at the crustacea. The latter were certainly a remarkable sight, being in all cases bi-coloured, the two colours contrasted and arranged in stripes and jagged lines, rather like the camouflaged dreadnoughts of World War I. There were many colours in the tanks: lobsters yellow and black, lobsters white and cerise, lobsters scarlet and orange, lobsters viridian and grey, lobsters sky blue and sienna brown, lobsters carmine and paint-box purple. There were scarcely two lobsters of the same pattern.

'What we have done is simple,' said José, rapping on the plate glass with one creative knuckle. 'Firstly, we have altered their genetic coding so as to transform their original vague colouration until we hit on strains which are the eccentric hues you see now. Then we bred them true, using cloning methods. Next, taking a clue from the colouration, we made use of research into orientation anistropy in acuity.'

'Whatever's orientation anistrophy in acuity?'

'Not anistrophy. Anistropy. It's an anomaly of vision. Permit nothing but horizontal lines in the environment of an infant mammal, and ever after it will have no neural detectors for vertical ones, becoming completely orientated on the horizontals. We found that the immature visual cortex of the lobster responds in the same way. See what I mean? The effect is on the brain, not the vision, but what happens is that, after the treatment we give the larvae in their visual environment, no striped lobster can see another striped lobster. Although they basically have the same nasty pugnacious natures as their terrestrial ancestors, they live together peacefully. For them as for us, it all depends how you look at things.'

'Very interesting,' said Edward politely. Then he added, 'Yes, that really is very interesting . . .'

'You get the implications for human conduct, eh?' said José. 'You see where my Tui thought came in? I believe that the culture matrix of our civilization – of any civilization – imprints us from birth so that we can only see horizontal lines or, in other words, only think along channels deemed correct by long-established custom.'

Genuinely interested now, Edward said as they walked back to José do Ferraro's office, 'I wonder if all the slightly differing environments of the zeepees will eventually give rise to a generation who are oriented to verticals or – to an entirely new way of thought.'

'My guess would be that we're seeing some such phenomenon already. It would account for all the cults springing up daily. I believe that Tui is one of the true new directions.'

They settled down in the office and José got them two pam-and-limes from the machine. As they were sucking, he said, 'So, what can I do for you, my lapsed friend?'

'Don't call me that, José. I still believe, but I've been so busy.'

'Ha, you're killing your spiritual life with work – you'll become a robot. The sad thing is, you know what you're doing . . . Well, how can I help you?'

Now that his moment had come, Edward was embarrassed. 'It's about a girl, José.'

'Good. I didn't think you were interested. Women are full of Tui-either-norness. Do I know her?'

'You may do. I believe she works here in FFFFA.'

'But you aren't sure?'

'It's an Internal girl, José. She comes personally to my place, but in disguise, of course. She has dropped clues about her real identity. For instance, once she said to me, "My happiness lies in artificial oceans". I made nothing of it at the time. This morning, it suddenly hit me that it could be the remark of a girl who worked in FFFFA. A reference to your seawater tanks. Then again, a remark she made about Chekhov convinced me she must be Asiatic.'

'Who's Chekhov?'

'How pleased you make me that I know some things you don't! He's a writer. Never mind him. You have a lot of Chinese staff here, haven't you?'

'You probably know that Four F A's fifty-five per cent Chinese-owned. Eighty per cent or more of the work staff are Chinese or North Korean. If your girl's here, she's one of probably two thousand. You'd have no way of identifying her, not if you've never seen her externally.'

Edward paused, then he said, 'Yes, I have a means. I think I have. I think I could identify her internally.'

'How can you do that? I've never heard of such a thing!'

'Nobody has. It's my own idea. And it's not unlike your

variable lobster idea. José, I've studied my Internal-girl through the eyes of the electron microscope plus the eyes of love. I've been down into her with magnifications in the millions, and I've seen something in her which no other human being has – her print, as individual as – no, far more individual than any lobster.'

'You mean – you don't mean a disease?'

'No, no, I mean her histocompatibility antigens.'

'Oh, the substances that set up immune reactions in tissue transplants.'

'Exactly. They insure that we are all immunologically foreign to each other, unless we happen to have an identical twin. They're sort of chemical badges of personal identity. There's a sufficient diversity of them to insure that everyone's antigen kit is different. It's the most basic form of identification there is.'

'And you know what your girl's kit looks like?'

'I have stills of her antigens. They're beautiful. I know them by heart. What's the matter? You're wearing your priest face!'

José do Ferraro was looking at him with a peculiar creased face, its expression seeming to alternate between mockery and affection.

'Oh, Edward, "Make simpler daily the beating of Man's heart . . ." Every day love reveals itself in a new form, as fluid and vigorous as Tui itself. Here you stand, enraptured by the girl with the beautiful antigens . . .'

Edward was touched by this speech, since he had not thought of himself as capable of rapture. 'You don't believe I'm being silly?'

'I didn't say that, did I?'

Edward laughed. 'O.K. Do an idiot a favour. Your welfare department must have records of all the girls employed here.

Can we run their medical data through a scanner? Under suitable magnifications, I know I could identify my Zenith.'

'Such records exist, of course. But it's illegal for anyone but the qualified Welfare staff to see them. So we'd better go and see Dr Shang Tsae, who works in Welfare – happily, his Side Job is acolyte to Priest Ferraro . . .'

XI

'I was worried about you. Wherever have you been?' Fabrina asked. No sign of the quarrel.

'Oh, engaged in a little private research of my own,' Maine said. 'I'm exhausted. Let me rest.' He walked over to the mirror and tried to pat his hair into order.

'Of course, my dear. Lin, come over here and tell your master a story. Make it a nice restful one.'

'All my stories are adapted to the mood of the moment,' said the lin, humbly yet smugly. 'This one is called "Dinosaur Inspector". "Taste the squalor of old obliterated airports," cried the dinosaur inspector. The people and incredible harlots were lusty upon the mountains. The dunes knew no spring. No animal eggs slept among the entanglements. But one strong man changed everything. Now bucolic perverts no longer lead the market. Falcons fly and magnesium bands play atrabiliously.'

'Not very cheerful,' Fabrina complained.

'I'm going to take a shower,' Maine said.

José do Ferraro had secured Edward access to the medical files of FFFFA, thanks to the illegal aid of Dr Shang Tsae. Then Edward had had to attempt his task of antigen identification without the aid of a computer – something for which he had scarcely bargained. He allowed himself twenty-five seconds to flip up each internscape in turn and scrutinize it. Even so, it was going to take him fourteen hours to get through the whole batch of two thousand, and sometimes he had to shuffle through several internscapes of one woman to get a clear view of the antigens. He tried to speed up his viewing; then fatigue slowed him again. The day had been fruitless, as predicted by his PM. He told the sober little Chinese doctor that he would return the next day.

XII

Early on the following morning, Edward Maine heaved himself from bed and padded over to the PM, letting it gather all his physiological data while he was still half-asleep. On depressing the read-out bar, he became fully awake.

**Key day. Persistence needed at start. Do not yield to impatience	
Antigen quest rewarded	96
Oysters yield great beauty	94.5
Increased heart-rate leads to precipitate action	94
Visit to the ever-punctual fly	79.5
Conversation delights	87
More initiative needed	
Outburst of invective can be avoided	77.5

Summary: happy day, partly enjoyed in attractive company

The second key day running. His life was certainly changing. One of the constant troubles he had had while developing the PM was that nothing ever happened in his life, so that in consequence the machine had nothing to predict; which made it difficult to tell whether it was working or not.

Now it seemed to be working full blast.

Just for a moment, as he dressed, Edward wondered how much the PM really told him. He could have guessed without its aid that this would be a key day. From the line 'Antigen quest rewarded' onwards, it looked as if he would trace his longed-for Zenith; but that also was expected. On the other hand, it was difficult to tell from the read-outs where the unexpected lay. There were displeasing implications in that last line, 'Invective can be avoided'. With whom? The machine could not tell him, or Heisenberg's uncertainty principle would be violated; it predicted the unexpected in such a way that it remained unexpected.

As soon as he could, he returned to the file-room of the FFFFA.

It was over half-way through the morning before he thought he had what he wanted. Before him glowed a remarkably clear shot of antigens in body tissue; they resembled strange deep-ocean sponges, and were brightly coloured. His heart beat at an increased rate. He felt his mouth go dry. In colour, in shape, they matched with Zenith's. He forgot that he was regarding a complex defence system designed to protect the human body from invasion by cells from another body; instead, he was gazing at a part of a world with its own perspectives, atmosphere, and laws which had no exact counterpart anywhere in the cosmos – an alien territory of beauty and proportion almost completely overlooked by man in his quest for new environments. By a paradox, this most personal view of his love was totally impersonal.

He turned to the file and read the name there: Felicity Amber Jones. Main Job: Marine Larvologist; speciality, Bivalves.

Felicity Amber Jones. Beautiful name. Of course, it was probably not her real name. The fashion was to adopt a name on arrival at the zeepees.

Whatever her name, it was Felicity Amber Jones herself he wanted . . .

An information board told him that Bivalves were in Level Yellow Two.

At Level Yellow Two, a preoccupied lady at a console told him that he would find Felicity Amber Jones along to his right.

Edward could hardly walk, so weak did his legs feel. His popliteal muscles trembled. He made his way along, clutching at a bench for support, face close to a range of tanks in which little agitated blobs of life flitted. Each successive tank contained water of a slightly different hue from the previous one. And in each, the blobs became larger and less agitated. In the last tank of the series, the blobs had come to rest on plastic trays inserted vertically into the water, and were recognizable as minute oysters. There stood a young Chinese girl in an orange lab coat, doing complicated things at a trolley involving small oysters and full beakers. She looked up at his approach and smiled questioningly.

He had never been in love before – not properly. 'Are you Felicity Amber Jones?' he asked.

She was in her twenties, a neat little figure with a slender neck on which was balanced one of the most elegantly modelled heads Edward had ever seen. The lines of this exquisite head were emphasized by a short crop of hair which curled round the back of the skull to end provokingly as two upturning horns. These seductive dark locks pointed to two dimples nestling under slanting cheekbones. Her eyes, slightly set back in her eye-sockets, were round and moist, being sheltered by dark eyelashes.

Didn't those pupils widen involuntarily, despite lack of any other sign of recognition, as she answered, 'Yes, I am Miss Jones.'

'Look, I'm Edward Maine.' He stammered his address.

'Oh, I see. Are you interested in our oyster-breeding? From pinhead to adult, it takes only fifteen months under our accelerated growth scheme. Here you see the algae tanks, each with a different algae table for different stages of larval growth, with temperature—'

'Miss Jones, you recognize me, don't you?'

She put a finger – the smallest finger of her right hand – curling it like a little prawn – into her mouth – receiving it between dainty white teeth – which were embedded in the clearest of pink gums – and said, 'Have we met before, Mr Maine?'

'Oh, yes,' he said. 'You're the girl with the most beautiful antigens in the world. I knew them instantly. You're the – well, you come to visit me at home once a week . . .'

Her gaze evaded him. Turning one shoulder – the gesture itself poetry – the shoulder itself a miracle – she made a little fluttering noise.

Standing on tiptoe in order to see her cheek over her shoulder, he said in a rush, 'Look, please – I know it's a terrible breach of etiquette – I know I shouldn't be here – but I've got a vacation on Earth – a whole month, courtesy of my corporation – and I can take along anyone I like – please, will *you* come with me? – I mean, it has to be you – you can name your own terms, of course – but please don't tell me I am mistaken – because you're too beautiful to be anyone but – Zenith!'

She turned back. With an effort, she raised her head – despair of any sculptor – and looked into his eyes – beauty of a Medusa – and said, 'Well, I may as well say it. You're right, I am Zenith. They'll sack me from the Internscan Union for admitting it.'

To his extreme pleasure and embarrassment, he found that

he was clasping her hands. Even worse, lit by artificial sea water, he was kissing her on the mouth.

Felicity Amber Jones proved to have just the shape and flavour of mouth of which he had always dreamed.

'I should be more formal,' she said, drawing back. 'Internal girls are not meant to behave so freely. Please do not try to kiss me again!'

'I'll do my best,' he said. He was not on oath. 'I feel I know you so well, Miss Jones, Felicity – Miss Jones. Now we must get to know each other in more traditional ways. You – you are so delightful on the microscopic level that I long to discover all the other ways in which you are delightful.'

'Please speak more formally to me during my Main Job.'

'Are you afraid the oysters will overhear?'

She laughed. 'Your average oyster is a very unreliable creature. It can't be trusted to keep its trap shut.'

'Then we must go elsewhere to talk.'

He was not sure exactly what to do with the girl when he had found her; her presence added to his usual confusion. But she was pliant and docile and readily agreed to any suggestion he made.

Despite which, it happened to be at her instigation rather than his that they found themselves in the Inarguable Paradise, the biggest of Fragrance's three fun-centres. The Inarguable Paradise had, as one of its chief attractions, The Ever-Punctual Fly. This Fly was a small satellite which orbited the planetoid once every fifty minutes. Unlike its parent body it had no artificial gravity; one of its chief attractions was the free-fall restaurant, in which delectable dishes were enjoyed while watching agorophobic views in absurd postures.

There were some other Chinese-Western couples here; such liaisons were common enough – at least on this zeepee – not

43

to excite comment; but Felicity Amber Jones declared that this was the first time she had been out informally with a Westerner.

'We call you "foreign devils",' she told Edward. 'The Chinese are at least as conscious of race and nationality as you Americans are.'

He found her mixture of directness and modesty both exciting and paradoxical. She was so perfect, her outline, her every contour, so clearly placed, that he was in awe of her. He wondered what her real name was – it was the custom with many people to take up a new name on arrival in the zeepees. His own terrestrial name had been Oscar Pythagoras Rix.

'Will you really come to Earth with me? I won't ask anything of you but your company.'

'Oh, that's quite all right.'

It was not exactly the answer that he had expected; yet he wondered if its seeming complaisance was more than he had hoped for. A premature gratitude flowed into the lagoons of his being.

He pressed her hand – opportunely, as it happened, for at that moment a quartet of Voivodina gipsies, specially imported from Earth, began a passionate lament to love, springtime, swordplay, Smederevo, the tide, innocence, moonlit nights, deserted churches, and a pair of forgotten lace gloves.

Edward did not tell Felicity Amber Jones that he had a commission to carry out on Earth. That might, he considered, make her less keen to join him. Instead, he concentrated on the pleasure aspect, unwilling to believe she could wish to come along for his company alone.

'What would you most like to see when we reach Earth? The glaciers of Alaska? Smederevo?' The wild music was still provoking his blood.

'Oh, I would love to see the reindeer herds of the Chinese

Arctic, grazing by the East Siberian Sea. I have never seen a reindeer, and they're so guilty and luxurious.'

'I've never seen a penguin. How about a trip to the Ross Ice Shelf in the Antarctic, to see the Adele penguins? You know they reproduce in sub-zero temperatures?'

'We mustn't concentrate only on cold regions. What about the warm regions? How marvellous to see Kilimanjaro rising from the zebra-trampled veldt and floating in the crumpled air.'

'How marvellous to swim in the Red Sea and wave to passing dahabeeyahs!'

'To take a trip to the Iguazu Falls, where Brazil, Uruguay and Argentina meet.'

'To jump into the chain of volcanoes along the spine of Sumatra.'

'To dive down to the new underwater city off Ceylon.'

'To surf off Honolulu.'

'Do you really know how to surf?' she asked.

'No. But I've seen guys do it on the scatter . . .'

XIII

When he returned home, the twenty-hour Fragrancian day was almost spent and a new one only half an hour away. Edward had held her hand on parting. They smiled at each other and promised to meet another day.

Now, like any callow youth, he cursed himself for not showing more initiative and kissing Felicity Amber Jones goodnight. Surely she would have allowed – wanted – it after such a splendid evening.

Fabrina was home with Anna Kavan. They were practising altered body images together, and becoming rather entangled. Fabrina stood up, blowing her hair from her eyes.

'We wondered what had happened to you. That reporter from Cairo is trying to get in touch with you again.'

'Only good things happened,' Edward replied, moving with nonchalance towards his room.

'So you are going to Earth, Edward,' Anna said. 'Aren't you fiendishly fortunate? You wouldn't like to take me with you, I suppose? I hear you have a spare ticket.'

He turned and confronted them both, drawing in his stomach and standing his full height.

'Not any more! You might both like to know that I'm taking a girl friend to Earth with me. It's all fixed, and I don't want any arguments.'

Fabrina threw herself at him. 'You fool, Edward, you fool! I can guess who it is – it's that little Internal-girl of yours, isn't it? You know nothing about her. She'll make your life a misery, you see.'

'Hope what you like,' he said, and escaped into his room. As the PM said, outbursts of invective could be avoided.

XIV

Next morning, relationships between Edward Maine and his sister were strained.

'What will you do while I'm on holiday, my dear?' he asked.

'I'd rather not talk about it. I'm too hurt. You don't care a bit about me.'

That killed that conversation.

The lin said, 'Neither of you is very happy. Let me tell you a story.'

'I'm perfectly happy, and I do not want a story,' Fabrina said, sniffing into a tissue.

'This one's called "Floating Airports",' said the machine, temptingly.

'No.'

'It is full of atmosphere and there is action on a meta-physical level. Also it features a strong tax inspector, together with some animals such as you like.'

'Oh, for god's sake, let him tell his story!' Edward said.

'Thank you. "Floating Airports". All over the old grey oceans airports floated. The towering sponsors walked drowning under deserted windows. And the tax inspector claimed, "Now all can sleep who cease to guard the leopards". So the strong officer went to the weak ruler and applied modesty. "Large export markets lead to decayed temples," one stated. So the animals laid eggs among the worldly.'

'Very nice,' said Edward politely. His sister did not speak. The lin bowed and retreated to stand itself against a wall.

For Edward, it was a busy morning, and one on which he embarked with some apprehension, since the PM's read-out forecast two embarrassing encounters. He went to Smics Callibrastics to sort out unfinished work, and was besieged by callers from other departments, among whom the most persistent were Sheila Wu Tun from Personnel and Greg Gryastairs from Kakobillis, who wanted errands run or messages delivered when he was on Earth. Edward was glad to escape at noon and go down to the travel agency, On the Scent, at Main Plaza East, to make his arrangements for the flight.

On the Scent were very helpful. He was booked aboard the *Ether Breather* in two days' time. The manager was somewhat awed by meek little Edward Maine, for the firm had given him a very generous luggage allowance. Kilo-costs for freight were so much steeper for the Fragrance-Earth run than for inter-zeepee trips, that anyone who travelled to Earth with more than two kilos of personal baggage was marked out as someone special; Maine, with his massive allowance, was a being apart.

The being apart was not content with his corporation's generosity, however. As usual, it had an ulterior motive. Callibrastics had prevailed upon him to take the prototype PM along, in order to do a field test in the more random conditions which prevailed upon the mother planet.

Slightly dazed by a pile of documents and brochures, Edward made his way from the travel agency to the nearest aphrohale parlour and got gassed on a nitojoy-pip.

As the heavy fumes poured into his nostrils, he heard the sound of musical instruments. A small religious parade was approaching, charmed on by pipe and drum.

It was a cheerful sight, bright even in the Plaza, which had been decorated for striking colour effects. Most of the people in the parade wore brightly coloured dominoes, complete with cloak and half-hood, and many of the hoods mimicked animal heads. Edward recognized the style. These were followers of Tui-either-nor and, if he had continued with one of his Side Jobs he would now be among them, complete with mouse-mask and a lust to convert.

Feeling guilty, he slipped back to a table at the rear of the parlour; which was a simple matter, since most of the patrons had moved forward to see what was going on. Religious belief was a participator sport in the Zodiacal Planets.

When the procession stopped near the parlour, one of its number, a well-built man in giraffe-mask and priest's insignia, began to speak.

'Friends, would-be friends, wouldn't-be friends, greetings all! Let me tell you what you're thinking right now. To some extent, you are aware of this procession. But you'll soon dismiss it: your mind's on trivial personal matters. It will be no part of you. Why not make it a part of you? You'll be richer. We're here to make you and Fragrance and the world a richer place.' The haughty giraffe face surveyed the denizens of the square.

'Do you know what sub-t or sub-thought is? It's a random pattern of thought which we all possess. It exists and is a measurable quantity. It has been denied in Western thought because it has no logic to it. That is why we have sunk into materialism. Sub-t can give you a rich spiritual life, with all alternatives open. This little procession can be your procession towards Tui-either-nor, the full thinking and spiritual existence. Espouse alternatives, or you will find yourself in one of life's cul-de-sacs.

'Only yesterday, my friends, I had an old acquaintance come to me in my Main Job – yes, like you I have to work for my living – I'm not a fake priest – and this old friend was in search of something. Once he was a member of this movement, but he reneged. He hadn't the persistence, the initiative required to follow what he believed in his heart. He had become a hollow man.'

Edward began to look about him, feeling warmth creep round his cheeks and ears. Eyes of frog, cat, leopard, hippo, marmoset, he sensed were on him.

'Yet that old acquaintance, my friend,' said the giraffe remorselessly, 'deluded as he was, he was in search of love, and love in a new form. He knew without knowing – he knew by sub-t – that his own spiritual life was dead, and he was driven to exercise fantastic ingenuity to look for a means whereby that dead life might be made alive again. There was a force in him greater than himself. You and I might think him a poor shrivelled creature, but all the while his life was being lived secretly for him.

'My word to you is—'

Putting two F-tallies on the table, Edward crept blushingly

away without waiting for the word. He felt indeed a poor shrivelled creature as he hurried towards the nearest trafficway. As he scrambled into the first carriage, his attention was caught by a message scrawled on the nearest wall: AMBIGUITY CLARIFIES.

Suddenly, he hated Tui. Life was difficult enough without emphasizing its difficulties. He was inadequate enough without anyone emphasizing his inadequacies. He could see why an earlier generation had turned away from religion and the spiritual life. It was too much for them.

What they really needed were fixed co-ordinates.

A predictable path through life.

No nasty surprises from sub-t or the collective unconscious or the endocrine system.

Just the dark glasses and white stick of certainty.

His immediate impulse was to go home, but he could not face his sister. Feelings still ruffled, he headed for Felicity Amber Jones's conapt, right in the heart of the urbstak.

Section Coty was a crowded place. Lower rates went with higher densities. He remembered that Felicity had said he should not come to her home. He pressed her signal all the same, and in a moment she appeared at the door, wearing a knee-length gown of cerulean blue chased with an embroidered electric design in silver. She wore a matching blue ribbon in her hair, which gave her an incongruously childish look.

Smiling, he waved the wad of documents at her.

'I've got our tickets! We catch a flight the day after tomorrow, Felicity. Can you be ready in time?'

She looked anguished. 'I live in a poor way here, Edward. You will despise me when you see how dreadfully I exist.'

'I'm not a bloated capitalist. Why should I despise you for being poor?'

'You know I had to take to being an Internal-girl. That's to support my brother, Shi Tok, who is an artist. He's here now. He lives with me.'

'I'll be glad to meet him. You didn't tell me that you live with your brother, as I live with my sister.'

She let him in reluctantly. 'He is very prejudiced against Americans, worse luck.'

Sharply, he said, 'Have you told him we are going to Earth together?'

Felicity covered her nose and mouth with a narrow hand and bowed her head. As she did so, a man appeared from an inner room, wearing a paint-stained shirt and smoking an absurdly small pipe. His hair was cut square, his face painted in stripes.

'What do you want?' he asked.

'This man is my friend, Shi Tok. His name is Edward. Edward this is my brother, Shi Tok. He is a great artist.'

'You probably don't care much for art, do you?' Shi Tok asked.

'Why, yes, I have a great respect for works of art – and for artists.'

'I see. The usual crappy worthless lip service. Why don't you get honest and say that you hate and fear art and artists?'

'Because he does not wish to be as rude as you,' Felicity said. 'Give Edward a pam-and-lime or something.'

'No, I'd better be going, Zenith. I can see I'm not welcome here.'

'Why's he calling you Zenith, Felicity? Say, Edward, while you're here, why don't you come and see what I'm currently working on? With all that enthusiasm for art, you might get a buzz.'

Despite himself, Edward found himself being pushed into a

small room where the three of them formed a crowd – perhaps because of the way in which brother and sister jostled and gestured, continually getting in each other's way – she trying to produce beverages, he to produce art-works.

The table was piled with boxes full of plaques. Another plaque stood in a vice attached to the edge of the table. Shi Tok spun the vice open and held the plaque out to Edward, who accepted it reluctantly. The plaque was a rectangle about the size of an envelope and not much thicker. It was cream in colour.

'I haven't finished that one yet. Know what it is?'

'Is it ivory?'

Shi Tok laughed harshly. 'I didn't mean what is it made of. I mean what does it represent. But no, of course it is not ivory. It's just a block of garsh, one of the new palloys. Ivory! Stars above! Don't you know that all the tariffs and duties stacked against the zodiacal planets by Earth make it almost prohibitive to import ivory to Fragrance? Not that I could afford ivory even at Mother Earth prices. I'm a poor artist, Edward, a creator, not a civil servant, or whatever secure dull little job you hold down – no, don't tell me. That sort of information makes me feel bad, puts me off my work . . . This is only a block of garsh, manufactured just a light-second away on one of the Ingratitudes. You know what it is?'

Since there seemed to be no answer to this question, Edward took the glass which Felicity offered with some gratitude and said, 'I'm not against art, although it's true I have a secure job. I'm a sort of artist myself, in a way – although perhaps not in a way you might recognize. What form does your art take?'

Felicity's brother looked upwards at the low ceiling and made grunting noises of despair. 'This is my art-form.' He waved the garsh under Edward's nose. 'And these boxes are stacked with more of them, masterpieces every one. Look!'

He stirred up the boxes, pulling out rectangular plaques at random. Each block had a band incised and painted across it. The bands varied slightly in width, colour and positioning, but there was never more than one band to a plaque.

'They're all named on the back, and signed by me,' Shi Tok explained. 'Here you are: *A Clutch of Underground Cathedrals, The Last Bite of an Unseen Shrapnel, Legs Trapped in an Embroidered Sea, Suntans of an Inoffensive Moon, The Spirit of the Male Climacteric Regards Narcissus, Friction Between Skull and Prisoner Brain* . . . Take your pick.'

'Um . . . do you sell these?' Edward asked.

'Of course I sell them . . . when I can . . . They go to rich dolts in your country or mine with more cash than brains. I rook 'em for what I can get. Like you, they hate and fear art, but they think it impresses other people, so I turn out this real junk for the pleasure of making fools of them.'

Edward sipped his pam and looked at the floor. 'Is it pleasurable to make fools of people?'

'They were fools long before I got to them. Why give them the real thing when they can't appreciate it? Art's as dead in China as it is in America. The artists helped kill it – they don't know what the hell they're doing either. The stupid oafs worked themselves into a dead end.'

Edward gnawed his lip and scratched his leg.

Felicity said, 'Edward is going to visit Earth soon,' and was ignored.

'Well,' Shi Tok said, throwing the plaques back in the box, 'why don't you say something? Don't you like my works of art?'

'It's not for me to say,' Edward muttered.

'Why not? I'm asking you, aren't I? You did come here uninvited, didn't you? What do you think of them, you a sort of artist and all that?'

Edward looked at him and felt a blush steal round his ears and cheeks. 'I think nothing of them, if you want the truth. Which appears to be exactly what you think of them. I'm sorry that you can claim to be an artist and yet know that what you produce is worthless, however much you get paid for it. You must be aware of the contradiction there. Perhaps it's that which makes you so angry all the time.'

The stripes rippled on Shi Tok's face. He raised a clenched fist, as much for emphasis as attack. 'I sell these for what I can get. No one respects the real artist these days. Even the lousy critics—'

'I'd better be going, Felicity,' Edward said, setting his glass down on the table close to the vice. 'Thank you both for the drink.'

'It's all very well for you to be superior, you don't suffer—'

She followed Edward to the door, despite the roaring of her brother. At the door, she stood on tiptoe and kissed him on the cheek.

'You're just wonderful,' she said. 'A real man.'

XV

Despite all the efforts to glamourize it, getting to Earth was just hell.

It started being hell at Fragport, where passengers for Earth had to go through long examinations in Customs, Medical, Expatriation, and Ecology, as well as the space line's Check In – where great exception was taken to Edward's PM, although he had all the requisite documents, and some small exception to his lin, which was only allowed through because it was an obsolete model (and he had only brought it to spite his sister).

Several people had come to interview Edward before he left Fragrance.

He was cornered by a plump shiny young man with a sharp-bladed nose, who shook Edward's hand and said he was proud to meet him.

'My name is Sheikh Raschid el Gheleb, and I lecture in Predestination at Cairo University. That's Cairo, Earth, of course. I've been trying to catch up with you for some while. Of course I am personally interested in your attempts to build a Predestination Machine.'

'Kind of successful attempts,' Edward said.

'So I understand. Spare me a moment of talk, please. What interests me is that Predestination is a pretty new thing in the West. Perhaps it is merely because I am Arab that I equate the outgoing capitalism of the West over the last few centuries with a firm belief in free will. The religion of the West, Christianity, lays heavy emphasis on choice.'

'Ah, the either-orness of Heaven and Hell,' Edward murmured, remembering the teaching of his Tui-either-norness phase.

'Now that Christianity is dying out and the West, faced with Chinese supremacy and the World State, has fewer alternatives, the peoples of the West – in the United States in particular – are turning more and more to predestination. This seems to me interesting, because the Chinese, in a sense, have always believed in predestination. So both sides of the world are becoming philosophically more ready for union. Do you see it that way?'

Edward hesitated. He liked discussions; they made him feel important; but he also wanted to board the *Ether Breather* and be alone with Felicity. 'No, Sheikh, I don't quite see it that way. The impetus that moves the West towards predestination is mainly scientific and technological. It's the running down of ready sources of energy which has given the average man fewer alternatives. Better scientific knowledge of the workings of the brain and the genetic system has simply ruled out the old notion of free will. We really are programmed – it is that knowledge that makes a PM possible.'

'I see, a diametrically opposed approach to the Chinese, in a way. I wonder if the Chinese will object to your turning what they have regarded as a philosophical outlook into a mechanistic one. May I ask you if your PM takes coincidences into account?'

'We are still in the prototype stage, you understand. But of course predictions can be thrown badly wrong by coincidence until such time as we fully understand the working of chance; there will then be no random factors, and coincidence will cease to exist, just like free will.'

'Do you personally believe in coincidence, Mr Maine?'

'Not in its old sense of a freak and rather unsettling concurrence of events, no. It is only under an Aristotelian system of logic that coincidences appear unaccountable.'

'Mr Maine, thank you. May we ask which ship you are taking to Earth?'

'We shall be on the *Ether Breather*. If you will excuse me.'

'I see – a real-life case of ether-or eh? . . .'

XVI

The *Ether Breather* had come in from the Tolerances, and was already crowded. Edward and Felicity found adjacent couches in the Soft Class lounge and strapped themselves in. There was a fifty-minute wait till blast-off; no foggers or sniffers were permitted.

'Shall I tell you a story?' asked the lin, ever-solicitous, from under Edward's couch. 'I have one called "Familiar Struggle".'

'At least the title sounds appropriate at the moment,' Felicity said.

'"Familiar Struggle". Bishop Cortara stood on heavy stone. "Struggle is as sure as death or spring: so be leopards while the high valleys flower." But the squalid photographers had heard too many promises. Musical weaving-mills burned. Pacific courts decayed. The pretty regiments came. He put his arms round a returning falcon and floated above the familiar windows of the Pacific.'

Edward fell asleep. When he woke, they were nosing out of the hangar in a mild cuddle of acceleration.

Passengers had the option of listening to music or of using the small screen-table before them either to watch a current film, generally Chinese or Japanese, or to view the panorama beyond the ship as seen from the captain's monitor. Most people opted for the film – *Confessions of the Love Computer* – but Edward and Felicity switched over to the spectacle of space.

Flying among the Zodiacal Planets provided a superb visual experience. The planetoids glittered all about, like a galaxy built of poker chips, their palloy hulls and domes giving them a high albedo. They circled Earth like a swarm of floodlit mosquitoes. There were hundreds of them, given life by the thermonuclear ardours of the sun.

Most of them had been constructed three and four decades earlier, in ambitious response to the Great Power Crisis. Energy was here for the taking – but energy always at a price. Many of the zeepees had been built under private enterprise, by large corporations of all kinds. At first, when enthusiasm was high and expertise rare, the failure rate was formidable. There were romantic tales of half-finished zeepees, of ruined zeepees, of zeepees unregistered at Lloyd's, of zeepees filled with water or poisonous gases, in which renegades and pirates lived; such things were the standard fare of scatter shows. Eventually, governments had stepped in when death tolls grew high enough to rouse public opinion. Later, groups of zeepees had formed alliances, often slightly altering their orbit to do so, and now governed themselves like so many city states.

Independent zeepees still existed; but they were mainly the poorer ones. Even the alliances fell increasingly into the hands of terrestrial nations as tariffs nibbled away their profitability. All came more and more under the Chinese hegemony. The Chinese owned – if only at second- or third-hand – the essential space routes and most of the space lines. Chinese artefacts and fashions ruled increasingly on even the most strenuously independent zeepees.

There were pessimists who claimed that the great days of the Zodiacal Planets were already over. Optimists claimed that the great days had hardly begun, and that the time would come when zeepees equipped themselves with their own fleets – a nucleus existed already – and towed themselves to new orbits round Venus, away from terrestrial interference. Nonsense, said the pessimists (who as usual in these cases called themselves realists); in a cytherean orbit, solar emissions would prove lethal and, in any case, the zeepees were only economically viable as it was because they were not too far from Earth. We don't need Earth any more, cried the optimists. The day will come, said the realists, when all our beautiful new worlds will float silent and deserted about the mother planet, stripped of their luxury and machineries – and that in our lifetime. Never, said the optimists, upping their insurance.

'We're lucky to be the generation that enjoys all this beauty,'

Edward said. 'But I'm looking forward to the sight of an Earth landscape again. To gazing at distant horizons. Myopia has become such a fashionable zeepee complaint. Of course, much will have altered since I was there last, because of the energy shortage. It's fifteen years in my case.'

'Only five in mine, but things will have changed,' Felicity said. 'Do you know what they have now? Sailing ships again! Big ones!'

'So I heard.'

'They are so short of horsepower. One horsepower will shift only one kilo in the air or nine kilos on land, but over five thousand kilos by water. So now all cargoes go by the oceans, just as in earlier centuries. In Shanghai and Canton, the shipyards have built huge windjammers with five masts which travel at seventeen knots – as fast as the old mammoth tankers.'

'They must need huge crews. The profession of sailor has returned.'

'No, it hasn't, Edward. These windjammers are quite solitary, with no crew aboard except just one technician. The constant sail-changing is now fully automated and controlled by computer in response to weather-readings taken on-ship and from weathersats. Isn't that romantic – those great white ships sailing the oceans all alone, each managing its own lonely course?'

'Marvellous!' he said. 'Like albatrosses . . .' He sat relishing the picture she conjured up in his mind, thinking how much of life he had missed by his concentration on work for Callibrastics. And he thought too of a model yacht he had had as a boy. He launched it on a pond near home and it sailed to the far bank, with a brave wooden sailor standing by its mast.

Brian Aldiss

'I'd really like to see one of those ships,' he said. Oh, the early days of life, before the machineries of the brain took charge. The dragon-haunted seas of Earth and youth . . . A wave of poignance cut through him, so that he could have wept. In his early teens, he had once loved a girl whose father was a seaman in the navy. She had written him a mad twelve-page letter describing Montevideo, exorcism, the secret parts of her body, and many other interesting things, and then had disappeared from his life. The oceans of the world were beyond all prediction.

Finally, he turned to Felicity, fragile in her couch, and gazed into her deep, dark eyes.

'We know such different things about each other. I know about you internally, but nothing about your circumstances, although I had the pleasure of meeting your brother—'

She burst into laughter, hiding her pleasant mouth with a hand.

'You hated my brother, just as he hated you! Why are you always so polite?'

'I was taught that one should be polite to Chinese girls.' He smiled.

She clutched his hand, giggling. 'Don't be polite much longer, Edward.'

He thought he caught her meaning. Turning to her hungrily, he said, 'Tell me more about yourself, where you've come from, what you want from life, what you think about, what happened to you when you were surrounded by real seas, not artificial ones!'

Felicity told him of a life lived mainly in the Province of Chekiang, of their holidays by the sea, of camping in the mountains, of her father's rise in the civil service, and of his promotion to Peking. She was most happy in Peking when

60

she joined a girls' Whole Diet Circle, which was established in a small rural township that was wholly self-supporting; there she had learnt fish-farming and other ecological arts. During those happy days, catastrophe overtook the family. Their mother became increasingly difficult, family quarrels an everyday occurrence. A favourite younger daughter was run over through the mother's neglect. The family polarized, Shi Tok siding with his mother, Felicity with her father. They felt scandal close about them. The father was given a post in the city of Hangchow but, in a fit of rage, he sent Shi Tok off to the zeepees to work for his living.

'And it was all predictable,' Felicity said. 'My mother was suffering from a brain tumour, as we should have diagnosed. She died suddenly, only a few weeks after Shi Tok had left home. My father became a very sad man, particularly when Shi Tok would not communicate with him, believing that mother's death came through his neglect. I volunteered to go and see Shi Tok, but it is expensive to travel in space and, with having to support Shi Tok, I might never have saved enough money to return if you had not come along . . .'

He tried to hold her story in mind, but his sense of injury won.

'You only came with me because you wanted to get back to your father!'

'That is not so, and I am very grateful to you. You know that; I have shown you.'

He remained uneasy.

Ether Breather was not designed for high stress. Its structure was built from various of the metal-plastic alloys. To get down to Earth, at the bottom of its steep gravity well, passengers had to change into a much stouter ferry.

Accordingly, they disembarked when they were 5,700

kilometres from Earth, alighting for a couple of hours at a duty-free way-station called Roche's Limit.

As they stood at one of the great windows of the way-station, looking out on the tremendous bowl of Earth below them, Edward said suddenly, 'I will take you to China. We'll go together. First, I must visit Cleveland, Ohio, to see my only surviving relations. You can come with me, and then we will visit your country. I have an errand for the corporation, after which we shall be free to do what we like.'

'Lovely, Edward! I will show you the ocean, and you shall watch the new breed of clipper ships sailing the China Seas!'

He clutched her and she did not draw away. 'That will be marvellous. First, I have to talk to a Minister in Peking, a man called Li Kwang See. It is important to get his approval of the PM unofficially.'

She gave a little squeak in the region of his right shoulder and buried her face in his chest.

'Do you know the minister's name?' he asked.

Felicity covered her mouth and nose with a narrow hand, shaking her head. 'Go on,' she said indistinctly. 'Why do you need Chinese approval?'

'We must secure Earth markets for full expansion. The World State will be in operation soon. Everything is getting very Chinese these days . . .'

'Only American things! Meanwhile, Chinese things are getting Westernized.'

Her voice was strained; he attributed it to the fantastic view before them.

'Even my little old lin is Chinese in origin.'

'I know – the very name Lin is Mandarin, meaning a fabulous creature like a unicorn, whose voice coincides with all the notes of music – melodious, you'd say!'

'My lin isn't much like a unicorn.'

'Maybe not. But it is symmetrical and beautifully proportioned, *and* it only appears when benevolent kings are on the throne. And those are legendary characteristics of our unicorns.'

'Aha! Then I like my lin a great deal, and will never part with it.'

They crowded into the ferry when it came, together with a flock of other passengers, happy that theirs was not a longer wait – unlike the zeepees, Roche's Limit worked by the twenty-four-hour terrestrial clock, and there were only four ferries a terrestrial day to and from Earth.

The nightmare of sinking down to the planetary surface. The choking moment of landing. The nausea of full gravity. The rank smell of natural atmosphere, full of millions of years of impurities. The horror of finding that they had arrived during that antiquated and inconvenient hiatus, night. The boredom of getting through Check Out, with its interminable examinations. The contempt at the antique forms of transport. The excitement of being together in this irrational, random world . . .

XVII

A week in Cleveland, Ohio, was like a cycle of Cathay. They left after only five days. It was true that Edward's old uncle was kind to them, and took them pedal-boating on the Cayahoga River. 'You'd never believe that this waterway was once notorious,' he told them. 'It was the first body of water ever to be insured as a fire-hazard. Now you catch big fish in it, and the duck-shooting's great, in season.'

But Cleveland itself was a relic when it was not entirely a slum. Its industries had died for lack of nourishment. Like most of the great industrial cities of the West, its inhabitants were villagers again, painfully feeling their way back to a rooted way of life.

There was no private transport. They caught an infrequent coach to the West Coast, waiting in San Francisco until they could get a passage to one of the distant Chinese ports. Eventually, they boarded a steam-assisted schooner, *The Caliph*, bound for Hangchow.

Edward Maine was anxious. A veil had come between him and Felicity. He did not understand, and feared that he had somehow offended her, so maladroit was he with women.

They had a fair-sized cabin opening on the promenade deck. After long arguments with their steward, Maine managed to get both the PM and the lin brought up from the hold and installed in the cabin. The familiar objects brought with them a sense of security.

'That makes it more like home,' he said. 'Lin, can you tell us a cheerful story?'

'America is disappearing,' said the lin, which was perfectly true. Already land was a mere blue line on the horizon. 'I have a story called "Deserted Dunes".'

'Would you like to hear it, Felicity?'

'I suppose so.'

'Leopards burned atrabiliously among the magnesium fountains. Musical girls walked among sand dunes because heavy increases in taxation were demanded. One old man said, "The ocean will return next year." Spring brought rain. Stone decayed. And again bells sounded along the deserted temples.'

She forced a laugh. 'Very cheering. "The ocean will return next year . . ." I wonder what exactly that means!' She looked a little green, as if the pitching of the schooner was having its effect.

With an effort, he went over to her and took her in his

arms. 'I know Cleveland wasn't too successful. This is the first time we have been alone together since Fragrance. The world distracts us . . . What the lin says means nothing – and nothing will return unless we seize it now. Oh, dear Felicity, I don't know what you really think of me – I know you really only came along for the ride – you really want to be with your father and never go back to Fragrance, isn't that it? – but I care greatly for you, and I want to know what you feel about me. Please, please, speak out to me!'

She gave him a look of – he took it for despair and something more. Then she broke from him and ran from the cabin. He followed, watching her run along the deck, her coat flapping in the breeze, a vivid figure against the tumbled drama of ocean. Then he went back into the cabin and shut the door.

For a long while, he sat on the edge of his bunk. Then with an effort, he rose again, beginning to unpack the parts of the PM and assemble them. *The Caliph* had its own wind-assisted generators, and passenger electricity was on at this hour of day. When the machine was assembled, he plugged it in at the power point and switched on.

The PM was not programmed with supplementary terrestrial data as yet. Edward realized more clearly than ever how far ahead lay the first generation of portable PMs. Nevertheless, the prototype should still be reliable as far as his and Felicity's personal situation was concerned. He was determined that they must disentangle that situation as soon as possible; the sudden lapse in their easy relationship was more than he could bear.

As the machine began to read him, he became aware of a queasiness in the stomach, a light film of perspiration on his forehead, the symptoms of incipient *mal de mer*. He tried to relax as the PM absorbed the levels of his physiological functions.

He set the machine to print out for the next twelve hours only. It began to deliver, its print finger moving with an irascible, jerky action common to machines and tyrannosauri.

Persist in your mission	
Anxiety precipitates crisis	76
Fragrance faces imminent destruction	99
Shock endangers love	47
Maintain contact with girl	
Further study of chance laws needed	99.5

Summary: multiple crisis in attractive company

Edward switched the machine off, pulled the plug from the power socket, and began to dismantle the machine, making a long face as he did so.

The PM was programmed for the confined world of Fragrance II. It had been fed no routine data since leaving the zeepee. Its prediction of catastrophe was a phantom, based purely on his current physiological state which, on Fragrance, would indeed have presaged some phenomenal disaster: here it presaged only possible sea-sickness.

'Maintain contact with the girl' was another plain nonsense, since on shipboard it was impossible to do anything else.

Unless – the thought came like a shot – Felicity fell overboard.

But it was a miserable little read-out, with crazy probabilities. And the 'Further study of chance laws needed' was irrelevant, since he had stressed such needs at every stage of research. The PM could not be expected to work in transposed environments without elaborate preparation.

He ought to dismiss the read-out, knowing how out-of-touch with reality it was. He was listening to a blind oracle, he told himself. Then he remembered that oracles were traditionally blind.

Searching the ship for Felicity in a state of anxiety, he found her eventually in the stern, leaning against a covered winch, staring at the horizon below which the last of America had disappeared.

'Don't stand here, my dear Felicity. It's too cold. Come into the cabin.'

The sails drummed above them. He put an arm tightly round her waist, taken again by her beauty, for all her present pallor.

She gave him a tortured look, then followed meekly. He kept one hand on her arm and the other on the rail. Noise was all about them, in sails and boat and sea, while his lungs rejoiced in the wild air. He was not going to be sea sick. There were minor victories of which no one knew . . .

Even in the cabin, with the door closed, they could still hear the gallant sound of sails and rigging. Felicity stood looking so helpless that he became angry.

'You've fooled me, haven't you? You came with me simply to get to Earth. I was mad to expect anything else. You don't want anything further to do with me, do you?' He ran his hands through his wild hair.

'Don't try to drive me away, Edward. What you say is not true.'

'Then tell me, for god's sake. Something's the matter. What is it?' He was shaking her angrily.

'All right, all right, you bastard! I'm not afraid of telling you – I'm afraid of your being unable to understand . . . You are going to visit Li Kwang See, is that so?' Her face was set. She scowled at him.

'I told you it was so.'

'Edward, Li Kwang See is my respected father.'

'Your father?' They stared at each other meaninglessly. 'Your father?' He did not know what to say. He went and gazed out of the small window at the hammering waves until he regained his voice.

'The minister is your father? Are you a member of the Chinese secret police, the Khang?' He turned to examine her. 'You were put on to me when my holiday on Earth was first on the cards. Your agents probably heard about it before I did. I was *tricked* into choosing you.'

'Edward, no, please don't think that. I'm nothing to do with the Khang, of course I'm not!'

'No? Wait – I know. It was that sneering thing Stein-Presteign said, moving me subtly towards you. This was all engineered by Callibrastics, so that someone would come along with me and see how I performed. Typical of them! You're paid by Callibrastics, aren't you?'

'No, Edward. I don't know anyone connected with your firm. It's just coincidence, nothing more. When you mentioned my father's name on the ferry to Earth, I could have died with astonishment. Literally, I could have died!'

'Yes? Then why didn't you say something then?' The tears in her eyes only made him more savage.

'I was just so amazed . . . I couldn't speak. I had to have time to think it over. But it really is just a coincidence. I cannot come to terms with it myself.'

He shook his head. 'You ask me to believe that? How many Chinese are there? Eight hundred million? And I pick on *you* by accident? I'd be mad ever to believe that.'

'You must believe it. I have to believe it. Or else I have to believe that you sought me out just because you thought I would help you speak to my father and win his favour.'

'Nonsense, I hired you by accident, through the Intern Agency! I didn't even ask for a Chinese girl.'

'Well, then, and you came to seek me out by devious means at FFFFA. *I* didn't seek *you* out. The advantage is with you, not me, and for me it's just as much of a coincidence as for you.'

'An eight hundred million to one coincidence? It's a trick.' Another thought struck him. 'You're lying, aren't you? Li Kwang See *can't* be your father.'

'He is, he is! Why are you so horrid? Your little scientific world's turned upside down.'

They continued to argue. They ate no meal that evening. Finally they fell into their separate bunks exhausted, and slept. The morning made no difference. Still they argued.

For a whole sea-week they argued. Sea-sickness never touched them, so busy were they with the problem.

'This is ridiculous,' Edward said at last. 'After all, I know a great deal more about the laws of probability than you do, Felicity. I cannot believe that this is a coincidence; the odds are just too long against it. It runs counter to everything in my theory of non-randomness – I'd be mad to believe it.'

'I'm fed up with your stupid little mathematical arguments,' she said wearily. She was pale and fatigued, huddled in the cabin's only armchair. 'You're mad to let a coincidence, however big, get in the way of our love.'

So exhausted were they that for a moment neither of them seemed to realize what she said. Then he looked at her again.

He began to smile. A great burden fell from him. She smiled back, concealing her nose and mouth with one small hand.

'Felicity, Zenith . . .' he said. He took her into his embrace, feeling her arms move about his neck as he kissed her, feeling her lips open and her slender body press against his.

'Oh, Felicity . . .' he whispered. They scrambled into the lower bunk, weeping and laughing and kissing.

XVIII

Edward never accepted the coincidence. By the end of the voyage, when they were adepts at love, he had come to live with it. But his mind still rejected it whenever the thought of it arose. It was as if he opened a familiar door and found that it led, not into the kitchen, but to the summit of Everest. It would always be there. He could not assimilate it.

Felicity adjusted more easily. As she explained, her view of life was in any case more random than Edward's. She positively skipped on to the Chinese shore at Hangchow.

The stinks and perfumes of the place amazed Edward, as well as its bustling life – private lives lived much more publicly than he was used to. He viewed it all with fascination and a little dread, realizing again how much of his urge to create a working PM stemmed from his own timidity, his suspicion of the new, the exotic. But with Felicity for guide, he felt entirely safe.

They spent that night in a small hotel overlooking the Grand Canal and next morning boarded a train for Peking. The train was pulled by an enormous steam engine and was spotlessly clean. As they waited in Hangchow station, little old ladies with faces wrinkled like contour maps of the Pyrenees sprang out of the ground and rubbed down windows and brass-work until everything gleamed. Then the express set off again through the great tamed tawny countryside.

To Edward Maine's eyes, Peking looked formidable, grim, and bleak, even in the fresh spring sunshine. At first it seemed like one more big monolithic capital, with its enormous squares, factories, and barracklike buildings. As they crossed Chang-an

Square in a blue trolley-car, the wide spaces made him feel dizzy; but Felicity effected a partial cure by showing him slogans set in coloured tiles into the series of grey paving stones. She translated for him, squeezing his hand.

'You young people, full of vigour and vitality, are in the bloom of life, like the sun at eight or nine in the morning. The world belongs to you. China's future belongs to you. Mao Tse-Tung.'

He liked the sentiment. It was still only nine-thirty, he thought.

The trolley-car took them past one of the great grey old watchtowers which had overlooked the city for a thousand years, to an older part of the town.

Felicity guided them to a small hotel in a side street where tourists rarely went, where the human scale was more to their taste.

'Oh, you will grow to love Peking, Edward. You see it was never a motor-car city, like the big cities of America and even Europe; so now that the motor car has gone, the city remains as it always was, without malformations. Wait till you get used to it!'

'I don't want to get used to it. I like it all as it is now – novel in every stone.'

It proved difficult to visit Li Kwang See officially. The Ministry for External Trade and Exotic Invisible Earnings was a gaunt grey building near the Tou Na Ting Park, its flanks patched by large-letter posters. It was eight storeys high and lacked elevators. Edward, clutching his letter of introduction from Stein-Presteign of Smics Callibrastics, took a whole day to work through junior officials on the ground floor up to senior officials on the top floor. The officials, dressed in grey or blue, were always smiling. One of them, greatly courteous – this was on the fifth floor, when Edward showed signs of impatience – said, 'Naturally, we realize that Smics Callibrastics is very important, both to you and to the planetoid Fragrance II. Unfortunately, in our ignorance, we fail to have heard of the company, and so must remedy that error by applying to a better-informed department. You must try to excuse the delay.'

He smiled back. The whole exercise, he thought, was beautifully designed to make him see matters in perspective. A Chinese perspective. He admired it, admired both the courtesy and the slight mystery – just as he admired those qualities in Felicity.

During his second day in the waiting-rooms and staircases of the Ministry of External Trade, it was revealed to him that the Minister himself was at present negotiating a trading agreement elsewhere, and that consequently the Ministry was unable to help him this week. They hoped that he would enjoy the simple pleasures of Peking, and that they might be able to assist him on another occasion. They presented him with a free ticket to a concert in the Park of Workers, Farmers and Soldiers.

'Oh, my father is so elusive!' Felicity exclaimed, when all this was reported to her. To relieve her feelings, she tore up the free ticket and scattered the pieces equably about the room. 'All these bureaucrats are the same. While you were languishing in that horrible building, I was speaking to some relations who live near here. They will try to trace my father. Meanwhile, tonight they invite us both to a feast.'

The feast was a glory in itself and successful as a social occasion. Among the multitudinous courses, many a toast was drunk to matters of mutual esteem, such as good health, longevity, wisdom, freedom from indigestion, prosperity, and the success of trading enterprises. Edward blundered home afterwards, holding Felicity's hand down narrow lanes, sharing his new knowledge of China with her.

'You see, this part of the world is better off than anywhere else on Earth. This is China's century, as one of your uncles said. I suppose the same claim could be made back in history. But now China has come out from behind her wall. She's been well-organized and peaceful for millennia – that excellent Shantung wine must have helped in that respect. Even during the purges in Mao's time, there was a tradition of forgiving and even welcoming back those who confessed the error of their ways. And no other country got by without mechanization on China's scale – India is a rubbish-tip by comparison. So now that fossil fuels and metals are as rare as rubies, China is not faced with the massive need to adjust which confronts the West. Why, take that gorgeous roast sucking pig we had – it never needed an internal combustion machine! That lobster in prawn and ginger sauce – it had never been near a nuclear fusion plant! You can't tell me that that stuffed goat's udder ever drew up at a filling station and found it closed for lack of gasoline! . . .'

They climbed laughing into their hard broad bed. He fell asleep with his head on her soft narrow breast.

XIX

A smiling, reserved uncle on a bicycle brought them word that Brother See was in committee at No. 35 Flowering Vegetable Lane.

Edward went there. The lane managed to look almost as rustic as its name, although new concrete houses had been slotted in an ugly way behind the walls which sheltered traditional homes of artisans.

It was evidently still necessary for him to get global matters into proper perspective. He sat out another session of waiting in a small upstairs room, looking out over concrete, grey-tiled eaves, dangling cables, a wooden house where two children played with a wooden doll, and a pigsty which contained five small porkers and a flowering cherry. He liked it.

His read-out that morning had told him he would sight his quarry today; but he remained sceptical of anything the PM said until he could feed it up-to-date programming. However, at three-thirty, a small procession of men in pallid business suits walked in dignity through the waiting-room. One of them had a face like a squeezed lemon and looked at Edward with a marked gaze as he passed; that would be the minister, Felicity's father.

My father-in-law? he asked himself. That would depend on how the interview went, among other things.

Mindful of his manners, he followed respectfully down the stairs. An old car like a hearse waited outside on the cobbles. A lackey sprang to open doors and the company climbed in. The hearse drove off.

As Edward stood watching it go, preparing to be at least a little angry, the lackey came up and offered him a small yellow envelope. He tore it open. Inside was a square of card. On it, printed, the legend: Minister for External Trade and Exotic Invisible Earnings. Beneath it in a perfect script were the words, 'Happy prognostications show that we shall meet soon in more harmonious surroundings'.

'He must have a better PM than I have, then,' Edward said, stuffing the envelope into his pocket. But the message pleased him, nevertheless.

When he showed the card to Felicity, she chewed the edge of it and puckered her brow in thought. To please Edward, she had gone out and bought a cheongsam, although she protested that the garment was wildly old-fashioned and, in any case, not true Chinese but invented in Manchester, England, for the benefit of the cotton trade. In this garment, as she lounged in a cane chair, she looked perfectly provocative. He went over and stroked her thigh.

'My father is a wily old fox,' she said. 'This is what I think. He did not expect that you would grasp all the implications of this message. But he guessed that you would bring it to me, and that I would understand it. The message shows that he is inharmonious here, therefore he wishes to get away for a while. You see, he prefers philosophy to trade. So he will go to our coastal house in Chin Hsiang, in the Chekiang Province. He has learned from the pedalling uncle whom you met that we are together, so he expects us both to join him informally.'

'It *must* have been more than coincidence that we came together. Otherwise how should I manage?'

'If you are grateful, then never, never tell my honoured father that I was once an Internal-girl and had men peering at the inside of my magnified private organs!'

'Shall I ever see those delicious organs again?'

'You will have to make do with your pornographic still photographs of them. So, let's pack up and go to Chin Hsiang.'

'It should be good there at this time of year. How far is it?'

'Only two and a half thousand kilometres by rail. A full day's journey on the train. Lin, you are very idle while in China, so you may tell us a story while we pack up.'

'I have a story called "Justice Performed",' said the lin.

'It sounds like a good omen for Edward. Let us have it in an alto voice this time. Proceed.' She gave the machine a mock-formal bow.

'Flight was impossible where perverted justice ruled. "Let us return with honour to the volcano," cried the lusty silver band of oldest harlots. "Let us build the weaving mills among the mountains." Next year, musical patterns led to familiarity. Falcons brought spring. Towering photographers performed before the strong ruler. Sleep came.'

'That's very sweet,' Felicity said. 'You know, Edward, it would be both politic and polite if you give a present to my father when you meet. Why don't you donate this antiquated lin to him?'

'It's worth nothing. I'd be ashamed to present him with something so limited.'

She smiled and said, 'Of the lin as of humans, the attraction lies in the limitations and in the maximum that can be achieved within those limitations. I hate my brother's toy paintings because he cowers within his limitations, but this lin is bold and imaginative within *his*, and my father would surely appreciate such a gift.'

Edward clapped his hands together. 'Then it shall be done. Lin, you are to have a more appreciative master.'

'We are all in the fiery hands of God,' said the lin.

XX

Chin Hsiang was a quiet agricultural town, built where two canals met. There were inviting hills to the south, their lower slopes sculpted into paddy terraces which flowed like living contour lines. The town itself was set partly on a hill. The modest house of the Li Kwang family was half-way up this rising ground, its wooden gate opening on a square. Blossom trees were flowering everywhere. Lying to the east, and tiny in the distance, was a bay of the sea.

'It's one of the loveliest places I've ever seen,' Edward

exclaimed. He went and walked in the square under the mid-day sun. There were a few stalls in the centre of the square, tended by stalwart peasant women, who offered gay paper toys, picture books, chillis and blue-shelled eggs and toads in baskets, pallid lettuce and withered tomatoes, huge radishes, bright green peppers, and little fish speared on reeds. Beside them were barrels and pots and colourful animals dangling on strings.

The whole picture pleased him. An ochre-walled lane led down from the square, a cobbled stair led up. The houses had tiled roofs. It reminded him of something, but of precisely what he could not recollect. He felt at home there.

That afternoon, they went to meet Felicity's father, the Minister. His bungalow overlooked a secluded courtyard shared by the main house. Felicity led Maine to a bare room at the rear of the bungalow, where a small fire burned. The fire was of sticks and peat; real flames played there, real ash fell. Maine, long accustomed to the mock-fire in his homapt on Fragrance II, gazed at it with astonishment; he had lived too much of his life between fireproof doors.

The delicate noises of the fire emphasized the quiet of the room. There was one window, which looked out at the court-yard without admitting much light. Beneath the window was a large desk of polished wood. Behind the desk stood a small man dressed in an old-fashioned grey suit. He made a small bow as Maine stepped forward. It was the official Maine had seen in the ministry in Peking, his face wrinkled like a lemon, his eyes guilty and gentle like a reindeer's.

When the ceremony of greeting was over, Felicity brought them some wine and the men sat down facing one another.

'There is something eternal about China,' Edward said, embarking with verve upon a flattering speech. 'I am very pleased to be here. Of all civilizations, yours weathers the ages best. You have accepted time as a natural element. In the West, time is a challenge. We've treated it that way ever since the Renaissance. The Renaissance has provided our great fund of ideas over the past few centuries. I mean the dynamic ideas of humanism, individualism, and speculations about the external world. You could say that the impulse which sprang from the prosperous families of Italy in the fifteenth century led us eventually to space travel, and so to the Zodiacal Planets, which are like little city states.

'But we're in trouble now that that questing spirit has brought about the exhaustion of fossil oil and mineral deposits. Some say that America and the West are played out. I don't believe so. But I do believe the times are temporarily against us, and that we are having to weather a storm of our own creating. Whereas China sails grandly on as if time does not exist.'

He paused several times during this speech, inserting gaps and 'ums', as he tried to remember what he wanted to say. He was not good at big theories, and had to recall what the eloquent Stein-Presteign would have said in similar circumstances.

'You are generous in your comments,' Li Kwang See replied. 'The strength of China lies in her land, and in the peasants that work it. There is nothing else. Possibly in the West you have been too arrogant with your land, and have not understood its meaning and importance. The big businessman has possibly been more revered than the small farmer, if I may so comment. However, as to time, let me relate to you an amusing incident which illustrates that time can stand still even in your ever-moving country.

'Whenever I am in Houston, Texas, I visit the elegant museum there to look at one thing and one thing only. That object is an eighth-century vase of the T'ang dynasty. When I regard that vase, the material and the spiritual come together and I am restored. The last time I was there, standing by the vase, a guide came along with a bunch of tourists, and he said to them, "This beautiful vase is thirteen hundred years old." Now, when I was there fifteen years earlier, that same guide announced to another bunch of tourists, "This beautiful vase is thirteen hundred years old." So, you see, time has been standing absolutely still in the Houston Museum for at least fifteen years.'

Edward wondered if he cared for the humour of foreigners, but professed to enjoy the story. He then produced the lin with due formality.

Li Kwang admired the curlicues of its plasticwork and Edward asked the machine if it had a suitable story for its new master.

'New master, I have an exciting story for you,' said the lin. 'It is called "Old Regiments". The regiments with goat eyes came among the valleys. Lonely old officers cried among the royal courts because taxation returned. "The export market is a dinosaur; it increases the flight from towering ideals," one said. But the magnesium airports changed towns. Volcanoes were built. Promises were obliterated. Girls put their arms demandingly round old fathers.'

'Very pretty – although we hope that exports are not necessarily in conflict with towering ideals,' said Li Kwang, smiling politely and hiding his mouth behind his hand.

'At least we can make part of the story come true,' said Felicity, going over to hug her parent. 'You see, girls put their arms demandingly round old fathers. Daddy, you must listen to what Edward has to say about his invention, the prediction machine, because it is very important for him that you approve of it. Tell him, Edward.'

So Edward embarked on an explanation of the principles

of the PM. He described how the prototype worked. He put it frankly that the PM represented a large financial investment, and that his corporation would be greatly assisted if they knew in advance that they would be able to export and sell the machine on Earth as well as among the zeepees – a matter on which he understood Li Kwang's word to be all-important.

For most of this speech, Li Kwang listened while gazing out at the courtyard, where a shower of rain was falling.

When Edward had finished, he gestured to his daughter to pour more wine.

'My word is a poor thing,' he said. 'You must not set too much store by it. Your invention sets great store by words. We are all aware of the power of words and must bow to them, but we should seek escape from their demands when we can. It is mistaken to fall even more into their power. Words must be staunched with silence.'

'Daddy, let us talk philosophy later. First, you must say yes to Edward.'

He smiled at her reproof, his face wrinkling into an even closer resemblance to a lemon, a humorous lemon. 'It is precisely because this is a philosophical matter that I am not able to say yes to our guest, vexing though that is for me.' He leaned forward and said to Edward, 'Mr Maine, you probably know that in China we already have a method of guidance for every day of the year. I will not call it prediction, but prediction is possibly a misnomer also for your prototype, seeing that it interpolates advice among its percentages. Our method of divination is based on one of the sacred books of the Orient, the *I Ching* – or *Book of Changes*, as it is known in the West. The *I Ching* is almost four thousand years old and still regularly consulted. It is a permanent source of wisdom, as well as a daily guide.'

'Oh, I know about the *I Ching*, sir, and I assure you we wouldn't want to put it out of business,' said Edward hastily.

'That is kind of you. Most considerate. However, the problem lies elsewhere. You see, your invention dramatically embodies a basic conflict between East and West, whether you realize it or not.'

Taking alarm at this, Edward said, 'I certainly do not realize it, sir. With the ability to see ahead a little, men should be less in conflict.'

'Allow me to make myself clear. Your machine is very elaborate in itself. It has complex diagnostic elements, and of course it relies on a power input. Then, it is not really effective unless its data is kept current by daily bulletins from a computer system, thus encouraging centralism. All told, it is most ingenious and will for that reason always be expensive and cumbersome; ever more pertinently, it will merely intensify the self-generating nature of Western technology – technology demands more technology.'

'But—'

'On the other hand, here is my modest divination machine.'

Li Kwang rose, turned to the north-facing wall behind him, and lifted a black package from a shelf set at shoulder height. He set this on his desk. From the same shelf, he took a container of carved cherry-wood, and placed it beside the package.

He opened the package, which was a book wrapped in a square of black silk. 'This is my copy of the *I Ching*,' he said.

He opened the container. A number of polished sticks lay inside. 'These are fifty twigs of the common yarrow, which I gathered myself in a Chin Hsiang hedgerow. They and the book constitute the world's best-tried method of divination.

'I need only these. Oh, I also need a little time and thought,

81

and maybe a little interpretation from Confucius. But that's all.'

Maine laughed. 'Without wishing to sound scornful, Minister, when our PM is perfected, it will cause you to wrap your book up and put it back on its shelf for good. A four-thousand-year-old book can't take much account of today's hormone levels, can it now?'

'Nor will your machine ever be advanced enough to enable us to grasp something of the sensuous cycles and rhythms of nature which shape our inner being, or help us to live in harmony with our surroundings, as does the *I Ching*.'

As he said this, Li Kwang slowly folded up the book and closed the box of yarrow sticks. He replaced them on their appointed shelf.

Maine told himself that this was merely a discussion, and he must not grow angry. He glanced at Felicity, but she had moved tactfully to the window and was staring out at the rain.

'Maybe our PM is a bit more accurate than your yarrow sticks,' he said. 'At least it works on a scientific principle. It's rational, it doesn't grow in hedgerows. Once we fully grasp the laws of chance and can predict coincidences, then we'll be almost one hundred per cent accurate.'

'And of course you see that as important. Yet in part you work on something called the Uncertainty Principle! Now that is very much how the *I Ching* works. The uncertainty is essential, forcing us to learn; otherwise we would all be robots, utterly predictable in a universe where every event is as foreseeable as a railway line.'

'You are making excuses for the inaccuracy of the *I Ching* by saying that. We do not excuse our inaccuracy; we aim to eradicate it. We want accuracy – and we're getting it.

What's more, we have only been working on this project for a decade, whereas you've had four thousand years!'

'Frankly, accuracy is one of the most destructive targets of the West. Also, you must realize that to work with devotion on something for four thousand years is very instructive, whether it is a rice field or an item of philosophical debate.'

'Yes, but if the concept is all wrong . . . I mean, I don't want to knock the *I Ching*, but I do know that the Chinese have claimed that it has predicted all the great Western inventions, like electricity and nuclear energy. That seems nonsense to me.'

'Forgive me, but it seems to me nonsense to say that the West invented electricity and nuclear energy. Both natural forces have always been around, and were around even four thousand years ago.'

'A slip of the tongue. I meant that we harnessed them. What I was going to say was, if you believe that the *I Ching* is true, that it functions effectively, then you should not mind the PM being sold on Earth, because it will not supersede your system. We maintain that millions of people who will live under the World State will be unable to use or believe in the *I Ching*, and so will turn to the PM for guidance. Besides, we are not in competition. If we make a little money, you do not lose it, because nobody makes any money from *I Ching*, as you yourself admit.'

'That is one great attraction of our ancient system. It is diffusive and not profit-cumulative.'

Maine gave up for a moment, and took a deep swig of the wine.

'May I ask if you got a prediction on our little meeting and how it turned out, Mr Maine?' Li Kwang asked.

'Well, you know this prototype is rather cumbersome; we

didn't want to bring it on the train, so we've left it in Peking for the time being. Eventually, we hope to get the production model down to the size of a small radio. But I'm sure it would have said, "Persistence needed, do not yield to impatience."'

Both men laughed.

'In the circumstances, I consulted the sticks to see how I ought to conduct our discussion,' said Li Kwang. 'My six sticks which I drew gave me the two trigrams of the Khien hexagram. Let me show you with match sticks.'

He drew a box of matches from his gown and from it extracted six purple matches with yellow heads. He lined them up neatly together, parallel and not touching.

'There you are, the Khien hexagram. Six long sticks. No need to break a single match.'

'What does it mean?'

'It symbolizes a lot of things. This undivided stick being lowest represents a dragon hidden. That is to say, it is not a time for activity. Maybe that signifies my coming to Chin Hsiang for a bit of a rest.'

'Go on.'

'I should also say that the whole hexagram represents some great originating power from heaven. That surely indicates that *you* are being considered, having arrived from space. Dragons also represent great men, and this second line shows there is an advantage in our meeting. The third line is difficult and vague. It could indicate that much talk goes on over the day and that by evening apprehension remains. Taken in conjunction with what follows, it indicates that I should avoid what is error in my eyes. And so on . . . The dragon goes beyond the proper limits.'

'Is that dragon you or me?'

'It could be me. If I behave properly in respect to the demands made on me, then a proper state of equipoise and fortune will be reached. That is a reference to your request to sell your machine here, of course.'

Maine clenched his fists together. He longed to sweep the feeble little sticks away. But at that moment, a servant entered the room and announced that a light meal was served.

Li Kwang would talk only on general topics during the meal. He was smiling and polite, and received without emotion the toned-down version Felicity gave him of Shi Tok's behaviour on Fragrance.

'He sent you one of his paintings, father,' Felicity said. She produced it. It was one of the oblongs of garsh; a band of an intermediate brown had been painted across it. 'Shi Tok says it is called *The Benefits of a Fast-Paced Sleep.*'

For a long moment, Li Kwang studied the plaque. 'I shall look at it later and derive benefit from it,' he said. Then he went on placidly eating his rice.

When they reassembled after lunch, Maine was feeling desperate.

'May I say, sir, that I was asked to come and speak to you because naturally my corporation wants to know the size of their market before investing their capital. I was not happy to represent them in such a matter. My strong feeling is that we should now shelve this discussion, because it is premature. If you will permit, I should like to come back in, say, a couple of years, when we have a PM model which will impress you more than anything I can say.'

'Since you are frank with me, I will be frank with you. I will speak as your friend and as Felicity's father. It is not your machine to which there is a fundamental objection, but to the thinking behind it.'

'But you do not yet know how reliable it can be, whereas

85

– forgive my saying this – you demonstrated the vagueness of the *I Ching* just before lunch.'

Li Kwang bowed his head. 'My daughter will excuse me if I make a philosophical point. Ultimately, it does not matter whether or not the *Book of Changes* is "true" in any empirical sense. Those who consult it value the way the book speaks to the older, less logical areas of the mind. It is a map to behaviour, not behaviour itself. Whereas you are producing, or trying to, a behaviour substitute. Further, it does not matter whether our map is "truthful" or not since, if all accept the co-ordinates, then the map becomes reliable through general concurrence.'

'Are you saying that if the map is inaccurate and leads you to fall into a ditch, you will all pretend there is no ditch?'

'No. I am saying that if all agree to believe in a certain god, then his power over men's minds is the same whether he exists or not. We do not believe in a god, but we have a belief in belief itself. That remains comfortably constant. Whereas you would be perpetually altering your procedures, adding new scraps of knowledge, new theories of chance . . .'

'Sir, that's not a valid objection. It simply means that new models would be needed from time to time – to the benefit of our clients, our shareholders, and the corporation. I hope your fundamental objection is not that we shall make money?'

'That is part of my objection, yes. All over America, to this very day, you still come on piles of old scrap automobiles or washing machines. And the useless motorways, mile after mile. All obsolete technology that exploited people in various ways to benefit corporations. In the World State, we plan to live in poverty, as China has always done. There will be no room for extravagant gadgets.'

Clutching his head, Maine groaned. 'You mean you're

actually legislating for poverty! You'll have a world full of peasants in one generation . . .'

'Ah, but in the second generation, we can build from a position of equality.'

'You'll drive out all the initiative to the zeepees. There will be nobody to build for you.'

'I'm sure you know the answer to that, Mr Maine. We shall build for ourselves. Nobody has ever helped us, and nobody has to help us now. Western know-how will be very welcome – but it will have to concentrate on the things that are real, and not on illusions.'

'You are looking at all this from a very Chinese point of view.'

'In case you think I am indulging in an idle East-West hassle, let me say that you could easily come to appreciate that point of view yourself. You admit that your attitude to life is not your firm's. One understands that you personally are not exploitive or aggressive, if I may say so – although you are a unit of an exploitive and aggressive society. I read in you characteristics of humility and endurance which would find ready welcome here. You should not waste them on a corporation which battens on your talents while secretly despising you.'

Maine stood up. 'Sir, I have taken up too much of your time. I can see that you are dead set against my invention and the capitalist society. I will report what you say to my Managing Director when I get home.'

'As you will. Can the lin tell you a pleasant story before we part?'

'Thanks, but no thanks.' He turned and left the room, marched out of the front door, through the yard, and into the road. The rain had stopped and the late afternoon sun shone brightly. He walked briskly to the square. As he went, he heard running steps behind him. Presently, Felicity caught up with him and took his arm.

'Oh, Edward, father has made you angry! I'm so sorry! He didn't say a definite No. You should have discussed longer with him and reached an accommodation.'

'I'm sorry, Felicity, I don't want to talk about it. Of all the stubborn and difficult old – oh, I know it wasn't up to him personally. He was just speaking as a Minister. Jees, how hide-bound can you get? This is just too difficult to believe, Felicity. I mean even fifty years ago I might have expected to meet up with such awful anti-Western nonsense . . . and all that old crap about the mystique of China . . . China! What's so special about China? How's it any different from America?'

'Some say that the Americans raped their continent, whereas we have always had to serve or be raped by ours.'

'Whose side are you on?' he asked, and then broke into angry laughter. 'Let's get away for a while. My head's bursting. Let's go and look at the sea.'

'It's farther than you think. It may be dark before we get there.'

'Stop talking in that defeatist Chinese fashion. Let's go.'

They took the ochre-walled lane down from the square, and came along by one of the canals. Then the track took them away among the fields. They climbed a hill where slack-eyed peasant women walked home pushing babies and wood on the handlebars of their bicycles. Where merging tracks joined, an aged man sat by a small locker on wheels, a paper umbrella above his head. Felicity bought two ice creams from him, but Edward was nervous of his and threw it away.

As they climbed the slope, planting their feet firmly on the well-trodden ochre soil, Edward said, 'You know what will happen? I can predict quite easily. In a way, your father's view makes sense; I have to admit it. His is basically the view of conservative people everywhere. But, pushed to its logical conclusion, such a view stifles initiative. The World State will kill initiative.'

'End of Renaissance?'

'Very definitely. China never had a renaissance, I gather?'

'We had a revolution.'

'Maybe your renaissance is to come . . . What is going to happen is that more and more positive-thinking people will migrate to the zeepees. And from there they will be driven outwards, to look for new fields to explore.'

There was a small silence. Then she said, 'My father is not a fool. He knows that what you call positive-thinking people always move outwards. He relies on that.'

'He has a funny way of showing it.'

'He has the only way of showing it. Men have dreamed of a World State for centuries. Now it is coming. It must have time to settle down, to get into working order. For a while, it needs stasis rather than progress. How can you achieve that without smothering the progressives? Why, by driving them out. They'll survive and profit by isolation.'

'Like little city states,' he said. Irreconcilable points of view existed and were necessary: maybe what was unnecessary was that either side should lose by the conflict.

Their way was downhill now, and the sea glittered through spring foliage. As they trotted forward, they lost the sun behind the shoulder of the hill to their rear. The track took them round a copse of flowering tung trees, and the ocean stretched ahead.

On it were three sailing ships, their sails still tinged with sunset pink, although the water was grey.

'Oh, that looks so wonderful!' Felicity cried. 'That's what we came to Earth for!'

'Better than your artificial oceans?' He took her slender arm.

'Yes, and those are the automated windjammers I told you about.'

He counted the masts. Five masts apiece, most of the canvas out to catch the evening breeze.

'Heading for Shanghai or the ports of the Yellow Sea,' she said.

They stood and looked at each other as the dark came on.

'Do you think your father understands as much as you claim he does – that Western ideas are vitally necessary to mankind?'

'I'm sure he read it in his Khien hexagram. It is a fundamental truth that most wise people have always realized: East and West are necessary to each other, like yin and yang.'

'Now you are speaking metaphorically.'

She shook her head. 'No, I was speaking personally, if you must know.'

They lay down together on the edge of the cliff, and dark came on.

Out to sea, the sailing ships faded away, heading for unknown harbours. Overhead, as the sky darkened, the stars began to spread. Venus stood out sharply, and then the familiar constellations. But far eclipsing them was a great halo going clear into distance, comprising hundreds of brilliant points of light. The darker the sky grew, the more brightly the Zodiacal Planets shone, ringing in the Earth.

The World State would come into being. Every night, the eyes of its citizens would be directed upwards, above the hayricks and the sullen chimney-tops.